Reluctant Romantics

"I don't think we have any more to say to each other, do we?"

"Well, of course we do!" The viscount ran his fingers through his hair and wondered when Frederica had become such an infuriating young woman. As a child he had liked her a great deal. But visions of Frederica the child vanished as he glared at the woman who had taken her place. "I have to say, will you marry me?"

To the viscount's horror two large tears gathered in her violet eyes and rolled down her cheeks as she staggered to a nearby chair and sank into it.

"Oh, Anthony!" she said, her lower lip trembling. "How *could* you?"

"Well, you don't have to accept! For goodness sake, Frederica—I've done my part by asking you. Now you do your part by refusing me!"

"But I can't—because—because Papa says . . ."

She stopped and glared at him. "I think it very bad of you to offer for me, Anthony, when not two minutes ago you said you wouldn't ask me to marry you if I were the last woman left on earth!"

"Well, you said you wouldn't marry me if I were the last man in the country," he countered, "and you said what you said before I said what I said. So just tell me we will not suit, and I'll be on my way . . ."

LADY'S CHOICE

JUDITH NELSON

BERKLEY BOOKS, NEW YORK

LADY'S CHOICE

A Berkley Book / published by arrangement with
the author

PRINTING HISTORY
Berkley edition / June 1990

ISBN: 0-425-12129-1

A BERKLEY BOOK ® TM 757,375
Berkley Books are published by The Berkley Publishing Group,
200 Madison Avenue, New York, New York 10016.
The name "BERKLEY" and the "B" logo
are trademarks belonging to Berkley Publishing Corporation.

PRINTED IN THE UNITED STATES OF AMERICA

10 9 8 7 6 5 4 3 2 1

For Carol and Joel,
Patty and Duane,
Jan and George,
Susan and Frank,
who gave the first Regency party,
and are themselves a cause to celebrate.

Thanks.

LADY'S CHOICE

Chapter One

"Papa!"

The Earl of Forkham gazed into his daughter's shocked face. Her large violet eyes were staring up at him much aggrieved, and the earl gave a smile of grim satisfaction. He had, at least, startled her out of the meek pose she assumed for such sessions as these, when her father was bent on making known to her the error of her ways. She was usually just as bent on charming him out of what she termed either his "irritation of nerves" or "sullens." Hers was a pose he found most annoying.

Before his last pronouncement his daughter, Frederica Farthingham, her blond curls a work of art, arranged as they were in the ethereal fashion that had prompted one of her admirers to liken her to a water nymph, had sat, feet dangling, in the large leather chair she always occupied when her father delivered one of his famous scoldings. It was a chair that dwarfed her ridiculously and had been chosen with care by the lady to remind the earl of his daughter's delicate stature. The knowledge that her small body contained a large spirit was not lost to Forkham, however. This time, at least, he steeled himself against the feeling of protectiveness Frederica's diminutive shape in the large chair was meant to engender—and usually did.

The hands that had been folded demurely in Frederica's lap now moved restlessly through the air. Her eyes, which earlier had been raised in polite inquiry to his own, were wide as she stared at him in amazement.

"And don't you *papa* me," the earl continued, "or go looking at me as if I'd accused you wrongly. It will not do, Frederica. It will not do at all!"

"But, Papa—"

"And no *but papas*, either! This latest escapade of yours—"

Frederica, dismayed to find that her best injured-feelings-face had not moved her father, or even slowed him down, flushed and bit her full upper lip. Lowering her dark lashes to full effect, she gazed in pained innocence toward the floor. "No, no, Father," she protested, her musical voice pitched low to sound as pitiful as it was possible for Frederica to sound. Even to *her* ears that was not nearly as pitiful as might be needed. "Not an escapade! Just a little . . . friendly race among acquaintances—"

Behind her, her brother choked, and Frederica turned to glare at him. The movement brought the earl's heir to his attention, and the older man's forehead furrowed.

"Friendly race, indeed!" Forkham said huffily. "A challenge offered to the city's worst libertine—"

"Not the worst," Frederica interrupted weakly. Desperate, she tried to think of others who might deserve that title, but could not. It was just as well, she decided, that her father ignored her protest.

". . . in Hyde Park, with half the ton listening and the other half pressing them to repeat what had been said . . ."

Frederica's flush deepened. "Well, I could not help it, Father!" she cried, abandoning her innocent defense in favor of a more direct attack. "He said such insufferable things—it was not to be borne!"

The earl's face, red before, increased in color. "What?" he barked. His bushy brows beetled and his eyes grew dark.

"What do you mean? What insufferable things? If the man offered you some insult . . . if he dared—"

"Well, he *was* insulting!" The words were quick as Frederica sensed the wind beginning to shift in her favor. "The things he said . . . they were terrible—"

"*By all that's sacred!*" The earl's heavy fist crashed down on his desk. He hauled himself to his feet, leaning forward on the mahogany desktop to glare at Frederica's brother. "You never said anything about this! If that damned cur offered my daughter an insult—"

Frederica swerved toward her brother, her eyes flashing fire. "You!" she breathed.

George picked an imaginary speck of fluff from the well-fitting sleeve of his claret coat and yawned. "Ask her what the insult was," he advised the earl, his clear blue eyes avoiding his sister's.

Some of the frown left Forkham's forehead as he followed his son's advice. There was silence in the library, interrupted only by the crackling of the fire, until the earl, his frown once again deepening, said *"Well?"* in a voice that brooked no defiance. Frederica gulped and took a long breath.

"He said," she began, her eyes lifting to her father's face, then dropping. Her long, dark lashes brushed her cheeks in a manner that never failed to captivate her admirers. Peeping up at her sire, not even such an inveterate optimist as Frederica could convince herself he was captivated. She gulped again.

"He said," she told him, "that . . . that . . ."

The words seemed to stick in her throat, and Forkham, looking from one of his children to the other, strolled around his desk and stood before the miscreant. He leaned back against the desk, his arms folded across his chest. In a quiet voice that was much more terrifying than his best shouting one, he said, "I am waiting, Frederica."

Not liking the height advantage her standing father had,

Frederica rose too. It made little difference; she still had to look far up as she said, her chin jutting out in a gesture both her father and brother knew well, "He said that my Starlight is well enough for a woman but not anywhere the match of that rat-tailed gray he rides, and that . . . that . . ."

Her words faltered as her father blinked and shook his head, sure he had not—could not—have heard right. Instinctively the earl looked to his firstborn for confirmation.

George obliged. "He insulted her horse."

Put that way, in George's bored voice, it didn't sound the same, Frederica noted. She put her hand out to touch her father's arm, half turning to glare again at George.

"No, no!" Frederica said. "He said . . . he said . . ."

George waited a moment, his head on a slight tilt to the left as he considered his younger sister. When she could not seem to identify the right words, he shrugged and repeated his statement. "He insulted her horse."

The earl was having as much trouble as Frederica in finding the words he wanted. His mouth opened and shut several times as he looked from his first child to his second, but no sound passed between his teeth.

How alike the two were in coloring, Forkham thought, both sporting their mother's golden curls and fair skin. George had grown tall, like he and his wife; Frederica, who did not come to the earl's chin, took after her maternal grandmother. Both had clear gazes and intelligent faces. So much alike—except in temperament. If only, the earl thought, not for the first time, they were alike in disposition as well!

But where George could be depended upon to think and then act, Frederica always acted first and thought later. The earl, whose own behavior more nearly matched his daughter's than he cared to admit, had no doubt that it was just such conduct that had landed her in this, the latest in a long line of misadventures that were earning her a reputation among the ton as—he winced at the thought—fast.

Hardening his heart against the plea in her eyes, Forkham asked, "Is that true, Frederica?" His tone made it clear that he believed it was and was only waiting for her to confirm it.

Frederica sighed. Put so, how could she deny it? What George said was true. Yet he never could know the fury she'd felt at the baron's teasing, at the way he mocked her skills simply because she had been born female. The baron, she realized, had a way of knowing just what to say either to irritate or please; there was something about him that was both dangerous and intriguing. He could be so charming one moment and so provoking the next. He had one of the most wickedly witty tongues in London, and they had enjoyed some delightful sparring matches together, for the baron never made the mistake of assuming that the Lady Frederica had no brain. At times she liked him very well, but now . . . now she wished that she had not allowed him to come so much in her way.

"Well, yes." Her words were low. She saw the grave look settling onto her father's face and tried her best to dispel it. "But that wasn't all, Father. It wasn't just Starlight. It was the way he looked, and the way he sounded so smug, and the way he dismissed me—me!—just because I'm a woman! I tell you, it was not to be borne!"

Behind her, George rolled his eyes. Her father, gazing in his son's direction, could not help but nod. Frederica shot George a suspicious glance, but his face had resumed its expression of reserved interest by the time she focused on him.

"I am not interested in all women, Frederica," the earl told his daughter, his touch firm as he removed her hand from his arm and returned to his chair behind the desk. They had had this discussion before. "I am, however, very much interested in you."

"But, Father!" Again Frederica strove to dispel the air of gravity that sat like a heavy weight on her father's shoulders. "You're making too much of this—"

The earl held up one hand for silence, his face incredulous. "Is it possible?" he asked. "Do you really not realize that all of London is gossiping about you?"

Frederica managed a weak laugh. "Surely not all of London . . ." she began, glancing toward George for confirmation. Since the days she'd taken her first baby steps her brother had served as her protector and guide, a trusted confidant and champion. Surely George—

She was stunned when her brother's quiet voice answered, "They're placing bets on you in the clubs, Freddie."

"What?" She swerved toward him in surprise, sure she had heard incorrectly.

"They're placing bets on you," he repeated. "And not only in the clubs! Yesterday Grimsby came home with a black eye; when I questioned him, he said he'd felt called upon to defend your honor when the grooms of Lord Marcham and Lord Ogglesby were making their own little bets!"

"Grimsby was hurt because of me. . . ."

George watched the color drain from his sister's face and continued without remorse. "The bets are on whether the race will actually come off, or whether Father will stop it. And if Father stops it, they're betting on when you'll commit your next outrageous act! I understand that at White's some of the wildest young bucks have taken to betting on just what that outrageous next act will be!"

"Betting . . . on me?" It occurred to Frederica that she was tired of standing and in desperate need to sit down. She sank into the chair she'd vacated moments earlier as her father and brother exchanged meaningful glances.

"I never meant—" she began.

"We know that, Freddie." It was George's quiet voice

again, and a moment later she felt his hand squeeze her shoulder. Gratefully she reached up her hand to pat his, even as she corrected him with "Frederica."

"I never thought—" she started again.

Her father sighed. "You never do." The earl's fingers drummed in abstraction on his desk. "Now, if you could just be a little more like George, here . . ."

"Yes." Feeling heartily sorry for herself, Frederica sniffed away the tears threatening to form in the eyes to which at least half a dozen suitors had written painfully bad odes. "We all know George is the good child—"

Behind her, her brother snorted, and she felt his comforting hand leave her shoulder. "Cut line, Freddie," he ordered. "This is a web of your own weaving, so there's no use feeling sorry for yourself now."

"I didn't mean . . ." she started again, glancing up into George's eyes. Seeing the compassion warring with censorship there, she straightened, and the pride that had rushed her into accepting Baron Barnsley's odious challenge to her and Starlight's skill came to the fore.

"Well," she said, slanting a glance from her father to her brother and back again. "Am I to be sent home in disgrace, then? Back to Farthingham Hall for the rest of the season?"

She tried for a breezy tone, heedless of the quick frown it brought to her father's face or the warning light in George's eyes. "After all, you can't really send me to bed without my supper anymore. Well, I suppose you could, but what good will it do? I admit, I'll miss the excitement of the season, but if it salves the family pride to send me into exile for my crimes—"

Too late she was aware of the thundercloud growing on her father's face, and stopped. Behind her, she heard George shift slightly, and she knew she had made a terrible mistake.

"That is . . ." She made a quick effort to correct her error. "I imagine it would be better if I left town."

Her father had been threatening to send her down to Farthingham Hall each time he'd been displeased with her behavior since she'd come out three years earlier. When she thought about it, that had been any number of times. Still, a hasty scan of his face told her she shouldn't have put on such an indifferent front, when in fact it would bother her a great deal to be made to slink out of town in disgrace.

"It's not fair!" she burst out, dashing away an angry tear that would not be denied. "The whole town talking, as if they have nothing better to do! Betting on a lady in the clubs . . . they should be ashamed of themselves."

She saw the worry in George's face and the sorrow in her father's and choked on the hot words that wanted to pour from her. One, then two, deep, shuddering breaths allowed her to continue.

"I'm sorry, Father." Her words were quiet, her fair head bent. "I truly am. For the embarrassment I've caused you and Mother and George, and for the pain. If you wish me to go, I will. Whatever you say."

"Whatever I say." There was a wealth of meaning behind the words as the earl's face relaxed. On instinct, Frederica glanced toward George for enlightenment, but her brother had retreated into the shadows by the window and she could not see his face. Her throat tightened as she turned back toward her father.

"It may surprise you, Frederica, to hear that I am not going to send you down to the Hall."

Surprise her it did, and Frederica reacted in spite of herself. "You're . . . not?" she questioned, her eyes straying once again toward George. He remained in the shadows. Seconds earlier she had thought that word that she was not to be sent into the country would be the best news she could hear, but now something warned her, a feeling of tension that made the hair stand up on the nape of her neck.

"No." The earl shook his head, looking tired. Frederica, knowing she was the cause of that weariness, lowered her head and waited. "Your mother and I have discussed it, and we feel that if we send you away now, it will be difficult for you ever to take your place in the ton again. You have done too many things, Frederica. Harmless pranks, yes, but . . ." He sighed. "To be thought wild to a fault, my dear, is not the notoriety your mother and I wished for you."

Frederica's chin sank toward her chest. "I did not wish to distress you or Mama," she said.

The earl nodded. He nearly rose to put his arm around his daughter's shoulders but something made him refrain. "I know that, Frederica, and so does your mother. We both feel you mean no harm, but . . ." His words trailed off and he sighed. "We think that what you need is something to steady you. If only you had brought yourself to accept one of the many offers made you these last three years—"

Frederica waved away the comment with a "Pooh!" Her father's brow darkened again, and he tapped his foot for several moments as he gazed into the fire. What he saw there was indecipherable to his children.

Finding the foot tapping more unnerving than her father's silence, Frederica could not restrain herself. "But, Papa," she said, not waiting for him to speak in his own time, "if you are not going to send me to Farthingham Hall, what is it you wish me to do? To stay in town, quietly, perhaps? What . . ."

Her father's gaze returned to her face, and he had to rouse himself to answer her. "What are you to do, Freddie?" A small smile flickered across his face as she corrected him with "Frederica," then was gone.

"If only you *could* live quietly, but . . ." The earl shrugged. "No, my darling daughter, twenty-two years as your father convinces me that that is much too much to ask. Things just seem to happen wherever you go. It's as if you're combustible, my dear! I don't know why, but so it always has been."

He was gazing at her with great fondness now, and Frederica returned his smile, hoping against hope that his solution would not prove as terrible as she expected it might be. Her hopes were blighted by her father's next words.

"We have decided, Frederica—your mother and I—that if you are to be the talk of the town, it will be for another reason than that which captivates the ton currently. You, my dear, are going to be married."

Chapter Two

"WHAT?"

If the earl had succeeded in startling his daughter earlier, he had nearly floored her now.

"Married?"

For a moment Frederica was sure she had heard wrong. A look at her father's implacable expression convinced her she had not.

"But, Father"—one hand came out in unconscious supplication—"no one has asked me for . . . oh, at least three weeks! And I already told Lord Butterington I wouldn't have him, so . . ."

Her father gave a regretful shake of his head. "I know you did," he said. "And your mother so liked Butterington."

"Well, Mama should have married him, then!" Frederica fired up, only to cool quickly as her father's eyes narrowed. "Of course she couldn't, because Mama already got the best match ever!" She flashed her most cajoling smile.

Her father's forehead lost some of its lines, but he shook his head again. "It doesn't matter," he said, thinking aloud. "I don't imagine Butterington would have you now, anyway—after this latest little escapade. Terribly correct is Butterington."

"Well!" Frederica's nose rose, and her eyes were over-bright as two spots of red bloomed in her cheeks. "It doesn't matter, because *I* won't have *him*!"

Behind her, George chuckled. His sister, he thought, would go to the guillotine protesting that she get to choose the blade that severed her lovely head from its slender body. The earl, roused from contemplating his daughter by the sound, said, "George, I think you may leave us now."

An obedient George walked to the door. He was almost through it when he appeared to hesitate, then half turned, saying, "Father, are you sure—"

"You may leave us now, George," the earl repeated. George paused only a moment more, then was gone.

When they were alone, the earl turned his full attention to his daughter. "Frederica, my darling," he said, his voice so gentle that an unexpected lump rose in Frederica's throat. "You know that your mother and I—and your brother, too—wish only the best for you."

Frederica nodded and looked down at her nervous fingers, pleating and unpleating the folds of her soft blue muslin gown. "I know you do, Father—" she began. He continued as if she hadn't spoken.

"And you know it has been your mother's and my wish that you should find the kind of love in marriage that we ourselves were lucky enough to find."

Frederica gulped and nodded again, her eyes remaining in firm focus on the floor.

Her father sighed. "Your mother and I were lucky, Frederica. Although ours was an arranged marriage, it was an arrangement that has worked well. From the moment I laid eyes on Lucinda, I knew I wanted to spend my life with her."

Frederica chanced a quick glance up, and her face softened at the sight of her father, leaning back in his chair

with a smile on his lips as he talked, almost to himself, of
his love for his wife. "Mama is very lucky, Papa," she said,
her tone warm. The earl gave his head a slight shake and
returned his full attention to her.

"*I* am very lucky," he said, correcting her. Then he
paused.

"Your mother and I . . ." the earl said, his fingers
steepled across his stomach. "That is . . ." He paused
again.

"Your mother and I," the earl repeated as he rose and
walked around the desk to stand over her, "wanted you and
George to find mates and love as well as we have loved.
That is why, Frederica, we have not been anxious to push
you into a marriage you, yourself, did not choose. But now,
after three years out, you still show no partiality for any one
gentleman, and these escapades of yours grow ever
wilder—"

He stopped and leaned back against his desk, folding his
arms across his chest as his anxious eyes scanned his
daughter's face.

"Is there anyone, Frederica? Anyone at all who kindles
even the tiniest spark in your heart?"

Frederica shifted her attention from the floor to the wall
to the portrait of her grandfather, which hung over the
mantel, as she ran her gentlemen acquaintances under
review. Oh, she liked Jonathan, Viscount Luckham well
enough, she supposed, and Robert Smythley was a wonderful dancer. Before the baron had landed her in the basket
with his challenge, she'd liked him well enough, too, but
not to marry. Heavens! Not for that!

She shook her head and looked at the floor again. "No,
Papa. There is not." At her father's sigh she raised her head
and said that perhaps if she just put her mind to finding a
mate . . .

The earl's head moved from side to side with an emphasis
that made her stomach tighten. He wore a look of resolution

that Frederica had seen several times before in her life—and did not like. "You have had time, Frederica—time and more to spare. Since you have not chosen a husband on your own, your mother and I have chosen one for you."

Frederica made a rapid mental review of every young man to whom her mother had introduced her with such hope this season—and last. She felt her stomach tighten even more. "I've already said I won't have Butterington!" she reminded him, her chin coming up in challenge.

"And I've already said I doubt Butterington would any longer have you," her father replied, his chin jutting out a bit too.

Frederica's gaze was intense as she tried to read the earl's face. "I'd rather *die* than spend even one evening at tea with Lord Cuttleton, no matter *what* Mama says about his extreme worth," she informed him. "He is *dull*, Papa! Dull, dull, dull! And he spills snuff down his waistcoat whenever he takes it."

The earl, who also detested the worthy but boring Cuttleton, assured her it was not he.

Frederica's mind sought another likely candidate. "Oh, Papa!" she said, and the color left her cheeks. "Not . . . not . . ." She faltered, for she knew that not long ago a gentleman had asked her father for permission to address her and had been denied, for which she had been most grateful. "Not . . . the Duke of Barlingforth!"

The thought of his daughter married to the elderly duke, who had children twice as old as Frederica and who Forkham thought should have had better sense than to become enamored of a woman as young as his daughter, so startled and appalled the earl that he rushed his fences—something he had promised his wife most faithfully he would not do.

"No, no, my dear," he said, his voice soothing as he stepped forward to give her shoulder a reassuring pat. "Of course not! What monsters you must think us, to be sure!" Frederica, about to disclaim this statement, found that his next sentence strangled the words in her throat. "It is not an old man you're wanting, or we're wanting for you! No, no, my dear! It's Viscount Chilesworth! It's Anthony you're to marry."

Forkham, beaming at her in momentary expectation, appeared certain that the information that she was about to contract an engagement with one of the most eligible and sought-after young men in London would be much more palatable to her than the thought of the elderly duke.

He was wrong.

Frederica, after opening and shutting her mouth several times as she stared up at him, her eyes growing wider each second, astonished the earl by rising from her chair, walking to the fireplace, and staring down at it for several moments before turning to face him, her back as stiff as a poker.

"No," she said flatly.

The earl blinked.

"I'd as soon have Barlingforth," she said, and there was defiance in every line of her small body. "I'd rather!"

The earl blinked again. "I cannot believe that—" he began, but his daughter interrupted him.

"And I cannot believe that you and Mama would wish me—*me! your only daughter!*—to marry that . . . that . . ."

Words seemed to fail her, and the earl regarded her with still more surprise. "You always used to like Anthony when you were children," he protested.

Frederica sniffed. "We are not children now!"

The earl said that the actions of both Frederica and the viscount made her statement one to be disputed. At his daughter's indignant glare he continued. "As you know, Frederica, Anthony's father and I, when you were a babe and Anthony only five, one night over our cups drew up a marriage agreement."

Frederica, who had heard this story since her childhood, was not impressed. "I also know, dear Father," she reminded the earl, "that when you were both sober the next day, you tore it up, saying you would let your children make their own decisions."

The earl frowned. "Yes, yes." His voice was testy. "And we would have, too, if either of us had children with the sense God gave a chicken. But no—" He stopped when he realized his daughter was regarding him most peculiarly, and waited.

"Are you saying . . ." Frederica began, shaking her head as if to clear it, then starting over. "Surely not! But, Papa, are you saying you already have discussed this with the Earl of Manningham and that he—he—*agrees*?"

Her father nodded. "Of course I have discussed it with Anthony's father. We are agreed it is the very thing!"

The earl was calm. Not so his daughter, who watched him pull out his large pocket watch and inspect it with care. "As a matter of fact, I imagine Manningham is talking with young Anthony right now," Forkham informed her.

"What?" Frederica almost shrieked the word, and her father looked at her in surprise. Frederica was not known to shriek. To shout now and then, yes. But not to shriek . . .

"Talking to that . . . that . . ." Her mouth did not seem to be working, and she closed her jaw with a snap.

"Really, Father!" she said, her gaze carrying infinite reproach. "Is that what you wish for me? To be married to a rake? A libertine? The stories I have heard—"

She was interrupted by the glowering earl, who demanded to know just what she meant by questioning his judgment and that of her mother. He added, as he thought about it, that he also would very much like to know just what stories she *had* heard—and where she had heard them.

Frederica shrugged her well-rounded shoulders and said vaguely that such tales were bound to get about. Then a thought struck her.

"And you say that *I* am wild to a fault!" she charged, her eyes sparking as she confronted her father. "Yet you would marry me to Anthony, who is wild beyond anything, and you tell me all will be right and tight! Everyone knows he runs through money like water and is forever doing some foolish and outrageous thing; and I saw him in the park one day with a woman who is *definitely* not a lady, and even though Mama says ladies are not to notice such things, I do not know how we cannot, while as for—" Frederica met her father's eyes, thought better of what she had been about to say, and took another tack. "You don't like my betting on myself in a race with someone, yet Anthony can wager one hundred pounds on his ability to drive forty times through a gate with one arm tied behind his back—"

"Child's play," said her father, interrupting. "A young man sowing his wild oats. Nothing more. Besides"—the earl had bet on the young man's ability to make good his boast, and there was satisfaction in his voice—"he did it."

Frederica gaped at him. *"He did it?"* she repeated. *"Nothing more than a young man sowing his wild oats?* Really, Father! Then tell me, why is it a scandal when I bet on myself to race to Brighton—"

Her father shook his head. "Anthony is a man, Frederica," he informed her. "It is different for a man."

Frederica's color heightened, and the earl waited for the coming explosion. He did not have to wait long. "Of all the ridiculous . . . pigheaded . . . unfair . . ." She stalked stiff-legged back to her chair and threw herself into it, folding her arms across her chest as she glared up at her father.

"I won't have him." Her tone was definite. "So there."

The earl returned her glare. "You will," he said, correcting her. "Anthony will call upon you this afternoon to ask for your hand in marriage, and you will accept."

"I won't."

"You will."

"I won't."

"You will."

"I wo—"

"You will," the earl said, his brow as dark as his daughter's, "or you will retire to Bath to live with your Great-aunt Honoria."

Forkham almost laughed at the change that threat made in Frederica's face. Feelings of outrage, shock, and surprise collided and exploded in her eyes.

"Great-aunt *Honoria*?" Frederica echoed.

Her father nodded.

"In *Bath*?"

The earl nodded again.

Frederica gulped and considered. "For how long?" she asked, one finger stroking her chin as she gazed at the wall in speculation, her eyes half-closed.

"For forever" was her father's prompt reply.

"*Forever?*" It was all Frederica could do not to shudder. Buried in Bath with Great-aunt Honoria and her horrid little pug that nipped at one's heels and tore one's dresses. Retiring at seven P.M. and counting it a rare treat to spend one night a month playing whist with octogenarians.

"You would not!" Frederica cried.

Her father's eyebrows rose; it was apparent he would.

"But, Papa!" She started up out of her chair. "Anthony and I rub on each other like flint on stone! We have ever since— Well!" She realized she did not want to tell her father "ever since" when, and when he asked, she replied with a vagueness that indicated more than anything that she was hiding something from him. "Oh, ever since we grew up, I suppose!"

"But you have met him forever in company these past few years," Forkham pointed out. "And you always seemed to be smiling. At least I never saw you cut him."

"One does smile, Father." Frederica's tone was that of someone instructing a slow child in requisite politeness. "Anthony and I are invited to many of the same parties. We must meet now and then."

"I have seen you speak to each other—even dance—on occasion," her father persisted.

"When we could not avoid it!" Frederica's nose was in the air. "We would not, after all, wish to create a scene!"

The earl, thinking of the scenes that seemed to follow his daughter and Chilesworth wherever they went, worked hard not to chortle.

"But we avoid each other whenever possible!" Frederica continued. "Marriage between us will not do. It will not do at all!"

"You will learn to get along," Forkham told her, ignoring the rest of her statement. "It will be good for both of you."

Frederica, who had serious doubts about that, could only goggle at him.

"Good for us?" she echoed. "The last time I had words in private with Anthony, Papa, I very much wanted to shoot him. I swear I would have, had I had a pistol handy. How will it be good for me if I end at Tyburn as a murderess?"

The earl laughed. "Marriage," he told her, "will be steadying for you both. Besides"—his eyes twinkled—"Anthony is quick. He'll duck."

"Marriage," Frederica responded, ignoring her father's small—and, she thought, in very poor taste—joke, "will likely drive both of us to Bedlam." She stared stone-faced into the corner. "I will not have him."

The earl shrugged and made as if to pull the bell rope. "I shall instruct your maid to pack for you, my dear. You may leave for Bath tomorrow."

"He will not have me!" Frederica cried, half rising to stay her father's hand. "I am sure of it! No power on earth could bring him to offer for me!"

The earl smiled. "No power on earth, my dear?" he repeated. "How little you know of my friend Manningham."

Frederica gazed at her father with dawning hope as a plan started to form in her mind. "Tell me, Papa," she said. "If

I agree to wed Anthony if he asks me but he doesn't ask me, will I still have to go to Great-aunt Honoria?"

"He will ask you," her father replied. "He will be here at three o'clock this afternoon."

"But if, Papa?" She was coaxing, as only she could. She had risen now and placed one pleading hand on her father's arm. Looking down into her large, hopeful eyes, the earl covered her hand with one of his own and smiled.

"If he does not ask, Frederica," he promised her, "you may stay in London, unbetrothed." Her face was wreathed in smiles, and he felt compelled to warn her. "But he will. Be prepared this afternoon, my dear. He will."

With another pat to her hand her father turned and left the room, leaving Frederica in possession of the library and her whirling thoughts. She considered her father's promise—or threat, as it seemed to her—for several moments before dismissing it with a snap of her fingers.

"Anthony?" she said, eyebrows rising as she stared into the fireplace. "Ask me to marry him? Pooh!"

Chapter
Three

SO SURE WAS Frederica that Viscount Chilesworth would not appear that afternoon that she was able to bear her mother and her maid fussing over what she was to wear for what her mother persisted in calling "the most important event of her life thus far" with equanimity, if not enthusiasm.

"Don't you think the lavender gown, my lady?" Frederica's dresser said with a curtsy for Lady Forkham. The countess, her blond head tilted to the side, gave the question her careful and prolonged consideration.

"No," that good lady decided, eyeing with interest the artful arrangement of her daughter's hair as the maid's cunning fingers twisted a knot to the side of Frederica's head and let the curls fall forward on to her shoulder. "I think—yes, I'm certain!—the new rose silk would be better!"

"But, Mama!" Frederica made the protest without thinking. "My new rose silk! I wanted to save it for a special occasion!"

Frederica met her maid's surprised glance in the mirror and felt her cheeks grow warm as her mother tsked-tsked at her.

"Really, Frederica!" The countess's voice was gay, and she clapped her hands in delight. "If becoming engaged is not a special occasion, what is?"

Frederica met her mother's gaze fully, and her tone was dry. "Am I to become engaged, Mama?" she asked.

Now it was Lady Forkham's turn to blush, and she stammered a bit before sending Frederica's maid off in search of her best rose shawl, which, the countess declared, along with Frederica's pearls and pearl eardrops, would be the perfect accessory for the occasion.

"Really, Frederica!" Lucinda scolded as soon as the maid left the room. "You should not be saying such things in front of the servants! Not that dear Jane would repeat it, of course, but it might distress her so, to think you are not as elated as one might expect a young woman about to receive an offer of marriage from one of the wealthiest and most attractive young men in London to be! Of *course* you are to become engaged! Your father and I are quite decided—"

Frederica snorted. "Wealthy and attractive, Mama?" she repeated. "Don't you mean spendthrift and a rake of the highest order?"

"Frederica!"

The countess managed, with a bit of difficulty, to look amazed. "Wherever do you hear such things?"

Frederica regarded her blond-haired mother with fondness and giggled. "Oh, really, Mama!" she said. "Coming it a bit too brown, don't you think, when just last week you and Lady Markley were saying, over tea, that Anthony is one of the most wickedly delicious young men on the town today—"

"No such thing!" her mother protested before adding, aggrieved, "And why you must have been attending to that, when so many times I *wished* you to attend and you did not—" Realizing what she had just said, Lucinda hurried on. "You are very lucky, Frederica. Any number of young

women in this town would give their eyeteeth to have
Viscount Chilesworth offer them marriage."

"Well, they wouldn't have to give them to me!" replied
her ungrateful daughter. "They could keep their teeth and
take Anthony and be welcome to him! Frankly"—she
slanted a speculative glance toward her mother—"I don't
expect him to come."

"You don't?" the countess echoed. Despite her best
efforts to remain positive, Frederica's mother had her own
serious doubts on that subject.

Frederica picked up her powder brush and applied it
liberally to her face. "*I* wouldn't."

"You wouldn't?" the countess echoed again.

Frederica shook her head. "Would you?" She paused in
her powdering to study her mother's face. Lucinda nodded.

"Oh, yes," the countess said, her head moving up and
down with such vigor that Frederica, who, unlike her
mother, did not know the threat that hung over the young
viscount's head, was surprised. "I would. Really, I would."

"Hmmph!" Frederica tried to read her mother's thoughts.
"Well, we'll see. . . ."

She resumed her powdering only to stop again and turn to
face the countess fully. "Mama," Frederica demanded,
"there is more to this than I know, isn't there?"

Lucinda's eyes widened, and she looked absurdly guilty.
Frederica thought of how her father always said his wife had
a painful addiction to the truth and was terrible at telling a
lie. She smiled.

"I believe I hear your father calling me—" Lady
Forkham said, starting to rise. Frederica caught her hand.

"Mama," Frederica said, "what is it?"

"Y-your father," Lucinda said, stammering. "I must go
to him."

Frederica gave her head a decided shake, tossing her
curls, arranged with such care minutes before, into confusion. "You know as well as I that Papa is down in the library

with George, puffed up with pride and awaiting Anthony's visit. He is not calling you, and you can spend a moment longer with me. After all, Mama"—Frederica lowered her lashes to hide her eyes, only flashing her flustered mother a sideways glance that that lady did not comprehend—"if I am about to become an affianced lady, isn't there something you would like to say to me?"

Lulled, Lucinda sank back into her chair and regarded her daughter with love. The countess's eyes misted with pride.

"Oh, Frederica," she said, beaming, "how I have longed for this day!"

Frederica forgot about being demure and only looked surprised. "You have?" She realized her mouth was slightly ajar and closed it as her mother nodded.

"My baby daughter, soon to be wed. My beautiful baby daughter, who grew up to be the most beautiful young woman in London."

Frederica laughed. It was the first happy sound she'd made all day, and her mother's eyes misted further.

"You are," Lady Forkham assured her. "The most beautiful and the most spirited—"

"*Headstrong* was the word Father used." Frederica's voice carried that dry note again.

Her mother sighed, then brightened. "I daresay you shall like being married."

There was a great deal of hope in her mother's voice, and the lady looked crushed when Frederica replied, "Well I *won't*!" in a tone that defied argument. Lucinda argued, anyway.

"*I* like being married," the countess noted. The whole-hearted truthfulness of that statement made Frederica smile in spite of herself.

"Yes, but you are married to Father," Frederica replied, "who is not a rake or a wastrel or high-handed or odious and outspoken and forever prosing on about what a woman should or should not do—"

Frederica stopped, conscious of what she'd said. She felt her color heightening as her mother, forehead wrinkled, protested, "Yes, but, Frederica, when you were children, you always used to like Anthony a great deal."

"Children," Frederica informed her, "do not always have the best taste."

The countess's forehead wrinkled further. "Do you think not?" she ventured. "Now, I, myself, have always thought that children could spot the good in a person faster than anyone, but . . ." Her mind returned to her daughter's earlier statement, and she felt compelled to note that Frederica was quite wrong about her father; he had, more than once—indeed, times out of mind!—prosed on (and on and on and on . . .) about what a woman should or should not do.

Frederica, remembering her recent interview with her father, agreed and apologized.

Lady Forkham was not done. "Frederica," Lucinda said, considering what had not been said, as well as what had. "Have you and Anthony had . . . words?"

Frederica sniffed and did not meet her mother's eyes. "Not when I can help it, Mother, I assure you!"

The countess eyed her with misgiving. "Frederica," she demanded, "have you and Anthony quarreled?

Frederica sniffed again and informed the world at large that she was not of a quarrelsome nature.

Her mother groaned. "Oh, Frederica," Lucinda said, shaking her head. "When did this occur?"

"When did what occur, Mother?" Frederica's look was one of inquiring innocence.

Her mother sighed. "Now it is you who are coming it a bit too brown, my darling," the countess said, and the lilt she gave the cant phrase made her daughter stifle a smile. "I may have detected a certain . . . reserve between you and Anthony when I've seen you together in company. But I thought that was probably because neither of you liked the

attention the other was receiving from so many admirers."
The fire in Frederica's eyes suggested that was not the most
politic statement the countess could make aloud at this time,
and Lucinda changed her tactics, voting for the direct
attack. "When did you quarrel with Anthony?" the countess
repeated. "And what did you quarrel about?"

Frederica said again that she was not of a quarrelsome
nature. She added, after a few silent moments, accented by
the tap-tap-tappings of her mother's foot, that she had taken
leave to inform Viscount Chilesworth her first season out
that he was a prude and a sap-skull and she did not need or
want his advice, opinion, or *presence* in her life.

Her mother gaped at her. "A *prude*?" Lady Forkham
repeated. Tales of the more extreme of Viscount Chilesworth's excesses passed through her mind, and she blinked.
"A *prude*?"

Frederica was highly incensed to see her mother dissolve
into giggles, and glared at her. "Really, Mother!" Frederica's tone was indignant.

Lucinda continued to laugh. "Oh," the older woman said
finally, regaining her dignity with effort. "I *do* wish I could
have seen Anthony's face when you called him that."

Frederica grinned in spite of herself. "He was stunned."

"I can imagine." The countess wiped her eyes. "But
why?"

The grin left Frederica's lips and she fiddled with the
contents of her dressing table, giving them her full attention. "It was several years ago, Mother," she said, her airy
tone fooling no one. "Spilt milk. I see no reason to talk
about it now."

For several moments the countess gave her daughter her
careful consideration, then Lady Forkham rose and placed a
light kiss on Frederica's forehead. "You are looking lovely,
as always, Frederica," she said. "I am sure Anthony will
consider himself a very lucky young man when you accept
his offer."

"Mama"—Frederica turned a look of urgent appeal her way—"can't you talk to Papa? You always said I could pick my own husband."

Her mother sighed. "If only you had, Frederica." She shook her head from side to side. "You had so many chances. So many young men who applied for your hand; some of them very good matches. I did so hope . . ."

Her voice trailed off, and Frederica, touched, asked gently, "Hoped what, Mama?"

The countess gave a tremulous smile. "That you would marry for love, my dear. But there! *I* have always found dear Anthony quite lovable, and I am sure that . . . with time . . . if you just put your mind to it . . ."

Her words trailed away as Frederica all but wailed, "But I don't *want* to put my mind to loving Anthony! And I have *told* you that Viscount Chilesworth is an overbearing, odious, high-handed—" She stopped for a moment, searching for more descriptive phrases, and her mother smiled brightly.

"Well!" Lucinda said, turning away. "At least you are not indifferent to him!"

"*Indifferent!*" her daughter echoed. "I'd like to see him dropped in the Thames! Confined in the Tower! Banished to America!"

"Oh, Frederica!" Her mother turned back, much shocked. "Surely not banished to America!"

Frederica thought a moment and shrugged. "All right," she amended. "Send him to Ireland. That would be bad enough."

Her mother giggled. "Knowing Anthony, he'd find an Irish horse that could outrun all the others and he'd be back in London in no time, with racing money in his pockets!"

Frederica sniffed. "Gambling!" she said. "Oh, yes. It needed only that!"

The countess, who knew her daughter's own predilection

for cards, smiled. "He is indeed a sad case, my darling," she said. "You will be quite busy seeking his reform."

"Not likely!" Frederica's chin came up.

Her mother walked toward the door, where she paused. "Be ready when your father calls you at three," Lucinda advised.

Frederica's face was calm as she shook her head. "He won't come," Frederica said.

She sounded so positive that Lady Forkham almost wondered . . . Then the countess smiled. Viscount Chilesworth's father had more than one ace up his sleeve, and Lucinda knew without a doubt that he would use every card needed to bring his heir into line. "We shall give you the most glorious engagement party, Frederica." The countess's voice was happy, her eyes alight. "London will talk about it for years, wait and see."

She slipped from the room, closing the door softly behind her. Frederica turned back toward her mirror and picked up her powder brush. She held it near her cheek for several moments, then put it down again. Frederica bit her lip and stared at her reflection in the mirror.

"He won't—he can't—he mustn't—he *daren't* come," she said. Her reflection nodded in sober agreement but said nothing.

Chapter
Four

IT WAS NOT a happy Viscount Chilesworth who presented himself at the Earl of Forkham's mansion on Grosvenor Square precisely as the clock struck three.

Anthony's temper, never the most even, had grown steadily blacker since his conversation earlier that day with his father—a conversation in which the viscount had found himself at the utmost disadvantage. Viscount Chilesworth, unused to being in such a position, found he did not like it one bit.

Their meeting had started off well enough; or, if not well, precisely, at least in a manner with which the viscount was familiar. The earl lectured on his son's myriad sins and omissions; Anthony listened, his dark head tilted forward in courteous consideration of all that was being said. When his father hit upon an item Anthony had most particularly hoped would not come to the Earl of Manningham's ears, Anthony's emotion showed in the surreptitious tugging of his cravat. Other than that, his hands remained folded in his lap as the earl spoke.

When Manningham broached the subject of matrimony and its settling effects on wild young bucks, Anthony's cravat tugging had become more frequent. His face and demeanor remained calm, however; his father had extolled the joys of wedded bliss before.

But when the earl spoke of Frederica Farthingham as the bride he had chosen for his son, Chilesworth shot from his chair, took a hasty turn around the room, and paused before the fireplace to direct a look of incredulity toward his father.

"*Marry Frederica Farthingham?*" the viscount said in such startled dismay that it would have done Frederica's heart good. "Ridiculous!"

His father had smiled—the slow, silky smile that, although Anthony was now a young man grown, never ceased to make him nervous. It occurred to him that the earl was not joking in the least.

"Ridiculous, Anthony?"

The viscount scowled now as he remembered how his father had almost purred the words. Manningham had leaned back in his chair, regarding his son through dark, penetrating eyes. "I think not. Although, of course—" his voice had grown even softer, causing the hair on the back of Chilesworth's neck to rise—"I am not the expert on ridiculous that you are. We have only to look at the highlights of your life to know that."

Not caring to having his father even *begin* a cataloging of said highlights, Anthony sought to turn the conversation with, "She would never have me!"

Again that silky smile from his father. In spite of himself Anthony, known among his friends for his fearlessness, had gulped.

"I have reason," his father said, "to believe that she will."

"Preposterous!" The viscount had run his fingers through his hair in distraction and gazed belligerently at his father. "Not that it matters, because I won't ask her."

The earl's smile grew, and Anthony knew of a sudden what it was like to be the fox, backed up against a fence

with the hounds closing in. "I won't!" he said. The earl had
said that they would see.

Again Anthony's look was incredulous. "You may not
have noticed, Father," he said, "but I am no longer six
years old."

Manningham's gaze started at the top of his son's head,
and traveled slowly down to the tips of his boots. During the
perusal his eyes rested consideringly on the viscount's
cherry-striped waistcoat for several more moments than
Anthony thought necessary, and a pained look on his
father's face made the viscount pull his coat closer together.
After his careful surveyance, the earl allowed that his son
was correct—he was no longer six years old.

Relaxing slightly, Anthony found his relief short-lived as
the earl added, "At least, not in size."

"Meaning?" The viscount's chin was raised; Manningham regarded him through calm eyes.

"I have never thought you lacking in intelligence, Anthony," the earl said. "I am sure that if you put your mind
to it, you can divine my meaning."

The viscount flushed and hunched a shoulder, much as he
had as a child. Manningham almost smiled.

"Then I suppose I know how to take that," Chilesworth
muttered.

"I suppose you do."

His father's calm needled the viscount, who snapped,
"You may say what you like, sir. It will not make me offer
for Frederica Farthingham."

The earl lifted his right eyebrow, and his gaze shifted
from his son to the miniature ship sitting on the fireplace
mantel. "Do you know, Anthony," he said as if the viscount
hadn't spoken, "I have been thinking for some months now
that travel is very good for a young man such as yourself."

"Travel?" Confounded by the change of topic, Chilesworth's forehead creased. With more than a little impatience
he reminded his father that he had made the Grand Tour

earlier than most young men. The earl waved that experience aside.

"And family," Manningham continued. "Family is good for a young man."

"If you are talking about family in the form of a wife named Frederica Farthingham—" the viscount started. His father looked at him. It was a long, sharp stare that stopped the words on Anthony's tongue and, seeing his son speechless, Manningham's gaze grew milder.

"Actually, Anthony," the earl said, "I was thinking about my brother."

"Your . . . brother?" The viscount was confused. He knew from long experience that the earl never thought about his brother if he could help it.

"Your Uncle Edward, Anthony." The earl's tone was reproachful. "Surely you remember your esteemed Uncle Edward. Off doing good deeds and saving souls of those less fortunate—"

"Yes, yes." The viscount's impatience grew. "Of course I remember Uncle Edward. I also remember your saying you were glad he was off saving others, and not here saving you. What has Uncle Edward to do with—"

"I was thinking," the earl said, his eyes once again focused on the small ship, his tone dreamlike, as if he hadn't heard his son's interruption, "that it would be a very good thing if you went to visit your Uncle Edward."

"*What?*" Chilesworth's mouth opened and closed several times, but no words came out. The earl smiled.

"Uncle Edward," Anthony said, each word succinct, as if he were making a point he was sure his father had forgotten, "lives in Brazil."

The earl nodded. "Travel and family, Anthony," he said. "Just the thing. See how well the two tie together? A trip for you to visit your uncle in Brazil could be arranged very shortly."

"I do not wish to visit Uncle Edward." The viscount was looking at his father as if the earl had lost his mind.

"The trip could be most educational."

"I do not wish to visit Brazil."

"The climate, I understand, is salubrious."

"Father." Anthony placed his hands on the earl's desk and leaned forward, gazing down into the older man's face. "I am not going to Brazil."

The earl shrugged. "A trip," he repeated, meeting his son's stare with an enigmatic one of his own, "could be arranged."

"I have told you . . ." the viscount began.

His father overrode him as, leaning forward, Manningham said, each word even, "And I am telling you, Anthony. A trip could be arranged."

The viscount straightened and took a step back. His eyes held an arrested expression as he surveyed his father. After a moment a crooked smile glimmered as he asked, with real interest, "Are you thinking of shanghaiing me, Father? Sending me off without a by-your-leave but with your blessing?"

The earl's gaze was bland. "Certainly with my blessing, Anthony." The soft words made his son's shoulders tighten, and Manningham gave another shrug. "It is a big city, Anthony. The strangest things happen here. People disappear and end up somewhere else. It has happened before."

"Preposterous!" the viscount exclaimed.

Manningham smiled. "Preposterous." He repeated the word, as if it tickled his tongue. "Yes, that is as good a definition as any for life."

"Wha—" The viscount's shock showed as he took a few hasty steps around the room before returning to ask, his voice one of real surprise, "Have I sunk so far beyond the pale, Father, that you would actually have me shanghaied to Brazil, to be saved by Uncle Edward?"

Manningham's voice was quiet as he replied. "No,

Anthony, you have not." The relief that crossed his son's face moved him, but he did not let that show as he continued. "Not yet. And it is my duty as your father to see that you do not. Your way of life seems to grow ever wilder, and it cannot go on. It will not go on. You need something of substance to interest you, Anthony, something to occupy your mind and heart—"

"Uncle Edward and Brazil?" the viscount asked, such loathing in his voice that this time the earl did smile.

"You have another choice," Manningham said. The viscount looked at him.

"Frederica Farthingham?" Chilesworth questioned. When his father nodded, he replied with a loud "Ha!" and threw himself into a chair. Running his hand through his hair, the viscount frowned at the tips of his shiny boots as his long legs stretched out before him. "If you consider that a *choice*, Father—well!"

The earl pointed out that Anthony had always found Frederica the best of girls when they were children.

"Yes, well." The viscount continued his gloomy surveyance of his well-shod feet. "She grew up."

"Oh." Something in the way his father said the word made Anthony look up sharply, but Manningham's face was devoid of expression.

"She won't have me," Chilesworth said.

"Do you think not?" The tone of polite inquiry made his son regard him with suspicion. Manningham smiled. "I have reason to believe she will."

"Won't." The viscount was positive.

The earl, after watching him for several moments, said, with only a ghost of a smile, that he, like his son, was a betting man, and he would make the viscount a wager.

"A wager?" Anthony's head came up and his eyes brightened.

"Yes." Manningham nodded. "I will wager you that if

you propose to Frederica Farthingham, she will accept. If that is the case, the two of you will be engaged."

"And if she doesn't?" There was hope in the viscount's face, and the earl gave an inward chuckle.

"If she doesn't," Manningham said, "but you have asked her, there will be no further discussion of visiting your esteemed uncle in Brazil."

The viscount, suspicious of his father's offer, but feeling for the moment that there was no way he could lose this wager, rose and extended his hand. "Very well, sir, I shall ask Frederica Farthingham to marry me, as you wish. When she turns me down, we will have done with this discussion. Agreed?"

Manningham nodded, and Anthony departed, not able to resist adding, "She won't have me! You'll see!"

He did not know that his father, watching him go through eyes half-closed in deep reflection, had smiled and said softly, "Well, one of us will, my boy. One of us *certainly* will see."

Now, as Viscount Chilesworth beat an impatient tattoo on the sturdy oak door of Forkham mansion, his frown grew even darker. He resented the position he was in, resented the fact that while he was sure Frederica would reject his suit—of course she would! She had to! Hadn't she told him once before that she found him abominable? crude? rude?—he hated to give his head to her for washing. He thought of the pleasure it would give her to reject him. Heavens, she might even laugh. Then what would he do?

When that thought occurred, his mind would not let it go; she probably *would* laugh—would laugh that he found himself forced to come to her like this. If she did laugh, so help him, he'd—he'd—

He'd what?

He didn't know, but it would be dire. He was sure of that. *And what if she accepts?* His traitorous mind slipped *that* thought over the wall he had firmly placed to block it. He renewed his assault on the door, to the indignation of the butler approaching on the other side. *What if she accepts, just to spite you? It's not as if you can depend on Frederica Farthingham. Who knows what odd starts she might take into her head?*

The viscount's hand stopped in mid-knock, and he paled at the thought. His mind replayed the memory of his father's smile of calm certainty; the earl had said he had reason to believe Frederica would accept Anthony's offer. Viscount Chilesworth was backing away from the door just as the butler opened it.

"My lord," Higgins said, bowing as he waited for the viscount to enter.

"She won't have me," Chilesworth said, straightened his shoulders, and stepped forward. A startled Higgins pretended not to hear. Frederica's mother, watching and listening through a crack in the door to the sitting room where she'd been seated moments earlier, feigning concentration as she obstensibly worked at her embroidery, giggled, then put her hand to her mouth to stifle the sound.

If I were twenty years younger . . . Lady Forkham mused, watching the viscount follow Higgins down the hall. A moment later she blushed at the direction of her thoughts, though she continued to eye her future son-in-law.

The viscount was, as always, impeccably dressed. His forehead was creased and his eyes emitted sparks; it was apparent to the countess that young Anthony liked being told what to do no better than her daughter. Lucinda smiled.

From the top of his curly black hair to the tips of his highly polished boots, Anthony looked precisely like what he was—a leader of the young blades of the ton. He carried himself with that certain air of breeding that is part of any true gentleman—or lady. There hung about him, like an invisible cloak, a current of electricity—or daring or mystery—that was, Lucinda knew, irresistible to many ladies. She had seen too many misses' eyes light up when Chilesworth entered a room to have any doubts on that subject. Visions of her daughter's face came to mind, and Lady Forkham sighed to think that Frederica was not one of those ladies. . . .

The countess watched as Higgins, his tread stately, preceded Anthony down the hall to the library. The butler announced the viscount with all the pomp that might have been afforded the Prince Regent. When Chilesworth had passed from her view, the countess returned to her embroidery, her ears tuned toward any sound in the hall. It was several moments before she realized she held her embroidery hoop upside down—an error she made haste to correct.

Beyond the countess's view, the viscount's entrance to the library was greeted with enthusiasm. Forkham pounded Anthony on the back and gave his hand a hearty shake; Chilesworth cast his friend George a look of mute appeal. George took a quick step forward, offered his own hand, and suggested that Anthony might like to sit down.

"Yes, yes!" The viscount realized that the Earl of Forkham was exhibiting the same good nature shown by his own inestimable parent earlier that day. Sensing danger, Chilesworth almost groaned. "By all means be seated, Anthony! No reason to stand on ceremony here!"

No reason at all; Chilesworth's thoughts were morose as he seated himself in the big leather chair Frederica had occupied hours earlier. It struck him that Forkham was remarkably like his own father, and he wondered why he hadn't noticed it before. Not that they were alike in appearance. Forkham was sandy-haired, a large, barrel-chested man; the viscount's sire was dark and tall, well proportioned. The viscount's father's voice was soft while Forkham adopted a booming style. But Anthony, recalling his most recent discussion with his father, thought critically that he would just as soon be boomed at. He sighed as

Forkham seated himself behind his desk and folded· his hands across his stomach.

Watching that action, thoughts of their fathers' mutual assurance rankled, and he sat with a heavy frown creasing his forehead. He was roused from his reverie when the earl, having waited several moments, said, "Well, Anthony, no reason wondering why you're here, is there?"

The viscount's brow creased further, "No, sir," he said stiffly. "I don't believe there is."

It was not the most auspicious beginning, and Forkham cleared his throat. Best to go right to it, he thought. "I believe, then, that there is something you would like to say to me."

In spite of himself, the viscount grinned, a crooked little smile that was notoriously heart-stopping to many vulnerable young ladies.

"No, sir, there is not," Anthony said, sitting forward and meeting the earl's look with one of frankness.

George, standing behind him, made a strangled sound, and the earl seemed in danger of following suit. Forkham's color heightened and his chest swelled as he gazed at his visitor.

"But—but—" the earl spluttered. Anthony continued.

"But while there is nothing I would *like* to say to you, there is something I must." Chilesworth's tone and words were smooth and betrayed none of the emotions warring within him. "And that is, sir, I must beg your leave to pay my addresses to your daughter."

The earl relaxed visibly and sank back into his chair, eyeing the young man before him. Viscount Chilesworth was well known to him, both as the son of one of his closest friends and as a longtime friend of George's. The viscount had run tame in Farthingham homes since he was a child, and Forkham believed there was no real harm, and a great deal of good, in the young man. Anthony had, of course, been dipping quite deep at the faro tables of late, but that could be stopped; the earl could recall when the young man's father had done the same, and now look at the careful parent he had become.

Forkham gave a wry smile; he was not much given to reflection, but it occurred to him that he had become just such a careful parent himself, and he prayed nightly that Frederica, who was very much like him, would never hear of the more lurid of his own oats-sowing escapades. Of course, he had been a young man and Frederica was not. She often told him that was unfair, but there . . . it was the way of the world.

George and Anthony, watching the man in front of them, exchanged glances. Anthony, uneasy, shifted in his chair; the earl looked as if he were about to read his future son-in-law a scold along the line of the one the viscount earlier had received from his own father. Chilesworth was not sure he was up to two such lectures in one day.

"Father," George said, watching the earl closely. The earl did not respond. "Father?" Forkham, shaken from his reverie, gazed first at his son, then at young Chilesworth.

"Just thinking," the earl said, excusing himself. He leaned forward to survey the viscount. "Want to marry my daughter, do you?"

Chilesworth, known for his honesty, opened his mouth to deny that, thought better of it, and settled on a shrug instead.

The earl smiled. "I like your honesty, Anthony. I prefer honesty in all people, especially members of my family or those who are to be."

The viscount gulped and the thought paled his complexion a shade. The earl's smile grew. "Truth is, Frederica isn't wild about the idea of marrying you, either."

Chilesworth nodded. "I did not think she would be," he said. The words were so dry the earl could not doubt they held added meaning.

"My wife," Forkham said, his words coming slow as he

watched his guest for any clue, "informed me not an hour ago that you and Frederica have perhaps . . . quarreled since Frederica came of age."

The viscount raised an eyebrow and looked inquiring.

The earl nodded. "Frederica wouldn't say what it was about, either," he told his guest.

"No." A small smile played at the viscount's lips, and he looked toward the book-lined shelves. "I do not imagine she would."

There was a pause as the earl waited to see if the viscount would like to say more. When he did not, Forkham cleared his throat and continued.

"You will be wanting to see her, then," he said. It was a statement, not a question, and the viscount, who did not want to see the Lady Frederica Farthingham at all, sat still. George, shifting uncomfortably behind him, suggested that perhaps a drink—in celebration—might be in order first. The earl, glancing at his guest, concurred.

"The very thing!" Forkham's voice was hearty. He allowed George to do the honors and accepted a glass of his best brandy from his son, watching as a second glass, containing a generous portion, was handed to the viscount. When George stood with his own glass in hand, the earl raised his and said, "To marriage!" in his loud voice. Chilesworth, about to sip his drink, was startled and splashed the strong liquor onto his new blue coat. He made a hasty dab at the damage, rolled his eyes toward George, and gulped the rest of his glass.

"To marriage," echoed George, when it seemed their guest was not going to say anything. Anthony, recalled to his manners, met the earl's raised eyebrow and the quizzical gaze of his friend and said, the word faint, "Marriage." When an obliging George refilled his friend's glass, Chilesworth gulped the contents.

"To the union of our families." Forkham raised his glass

again. "You must know, Anthony, that this is something your father and I have long hoped for."

Anthony's nod was glum. He wondered why his parents had been blessed with only one child—himself—when a sibling might have been more attuned to the idea of matrimony.

George, watching the scene, could tell that his father could go on in this vein forever, while the viscount, tossing down the brandy like water whenever it was given him, might be happily cast away in less than an hour if the situation continued. Clearing his throat and giving a pointed glance toward the grandfather clock that stood ticking away the moments in the library, George suggested that his father might like to call Frederica. The earl, his mind on his long-standing friendship with the viscount's father, looked at him in surprise.

"Frederica?" he repeated. "What would we be wanting her for?"

"Yes." Anthony had a heavy frown for his lifelong friend. "What would we be wanting Freder . . . Freder . . . old Freddie for?"

George ignored Chilesworth and concentrated on his father. "I believe, sir," he said with a slight bow, "that Frederica is the reason for Anthony's visit."

Chilesworth snorted. "Well, she's not," he informed George, his mouth grim. "My *father* is the reason for my visit. Frederica is just the . . . just the . . ."

Anthony could not think of the word to describe what Frederica was "just the," and lapsed into silence, concentrating. The earl, roused from his own abstraction by his guest's strange behavior, raised an eyebrow at George and held up two fingers, to ask if the viscount had imbibed two glasses of the excellent brandy in so short a time. George, shaking his head slightly, replied with three fingers.

Surprised, Forkham hurried around his desk and took the glass out of Anthony's hand, clapping the viscount on the shoulder as he said that yes, yes, they'd send for Frederica immediately.

"No, no." Anthony's protest was polite. "Not on my account." He realized the earl was looking at him strangely, and straightened. "That is . . . of course. Glad to see Freddie. Came to see her, didn't I? I forgot." The earl's look grew stranger still, and the viscount appealed to George for help. "That is, came to see your father, because my father said— But knew I'd need to see Freddie."

"She prefers," George said, his voice gentle, "Frederica now."

The viscount gave a gloomy nod. "Of course," he said. He sighed. "Freddie was such a taking little thing."

"Frederica," George said, his tone still gentle as he crossed to the bellpull, "has a great many admirers." In answer to his summons, Higgins appeared at the doorway and George requested that a pot of coffee—strong—be brought to the library. At once. Anthony, trying to be helpful, said there was no reason to make a fuss about coffee; he'd be happy to go on drinking brandy and save them the trouble.

George grinned. "You'd perhaps had a glass or two before you visited us this afternoon, hadn't you, Anthony?"

The viscount gazed at him in dismay. "Dash it, George!" he exclaimed. "Are you implying that I'm castaway?"

George shook his head and thought briefly about shaking his friend. "No, no," he said soothingly. "But it's not like you to grow maudlin after a little brandy—"

"Well, it ain't the brandy," Anthony informed him, and his voice held a certain huffy tone. "Dash it, George, I'm about to become engaged. If that isn't a reason to grow maudlin—" He caught sight of the earl's face and stopped, hunching a shoulder. "That is . . . well . . ." Chilesworth sighed. "I did toss down a glass or two of burgundy, after I talked with my father, now that you mention it."

George nodded. "I think you had better drink the coffee,

Anthony," he told his friend as Higgins reentered the room, carrying a heavy, ornate tray on which sat a silver coffeepot and several cups. "Frederica is not likely to take well to you passing out during a proposal."

"Think she won't have me?" Anthony asked, his tone so hopeful that both the earl and George were hard put not to laugh. "Told my father she wouldn't. Well, stands to reason, after last time, but he said—"

"After last time, Anthony?" George questioned, carrying a cup of coffee to his friend. The viscount, collecting his thoughts, said it was nothing—nothing—and relapsed into silence as he sipped the strong brew. When he had finished the cup and George had poured him another, Chilesworth looked toward the earl and said, the question tentative, "You won't be too disappointed, sir, if Freddie—I mean, Frederica—won't have me?"

The earl grinned. "Disappointed, Anthony?" He tilted his head to the left and thought a moment. "Let us say, rather, that I would be a good deal surprised."

"You would?" Viscount Chilesworth was beginning to feel a great deal more sober, and this pronouncement added to his sobriety.

The earl assured him that he would.

"Oh," Anthony said, giving that deep thought. "You've threatened her, too, have you?"

The earl's grin grew. "Let us just say, Anthony, that I believe Frederica to be . . . persuaded to listen to your offer with an open mind."

"Oh." The viscount sighed, his speculation confirmed. "You've threatened her."

George, coming up behind his friend, suggested that this might be a very good time to summon his soon to be betrothed sister.

Chapter
Five

AT THREE P.M. Frederica Farthingham sat in tense anticipation on the end of her delicate gilt chair, staring at herself in her dressing table mirror. Although she told herself again and again that Chilesworth would not come, there was a perverse corner of her mind that insisted on reminding her just how contrary Anthony could be. He might, that perverse corner said, come just to spite her. That it would spite him, too, was the hope the rest of her mind clung to with fluctuating success.

She wished that she had sent her maid, Jane, to spy for her, and to apprise her instantly if a certain viscount had the temerity to show his face at the Forkham mansion front door.

For a moment she considered slipping out of her room to peer over the banister herself, but quick reflection told her she did not know how she would explain that action should anyone see her at it. Instead she sat, watching the clock on her mantel tick its way toward three o'clock and then—oh so slowly—past.

By three-ten she was ready to scream; at three-fifteen she was pacing, waiting for her father's summons and wondering if she had the courage to take on Bath, and

Great-aunt Honoria. At three-twenty, however, she started to feel better.

"He didn't come," she told her reflection in the mirror as she swished by. It gazed back at her hopefully.

By three-thirty Frederica was smiling, and humming a little tune. At four P.M. she had just reached for the bellpull to summon her maid when the woman scurried into the room, her face aglow.

"Oh, my lady," Jane trilled, her eyes dancing with excitement. "Mr. Higgins has sent me to fetch you. Your father requires your presence in the library—at once."

The extra nod and meaning behind the words *at once* made Frederica's heart lurch, and she paled. "At once?" she repeated. "In the library?"

Jane beamed. "Yes, my lady," she assured her. "Your father and . . . someone else!" Frederica could see that the maid was agog at the thought of the "someone else," and her heart dropped further.

"He came!" Frederica wailed, sinking down into her chair and pulling at her hair in such a way as to cause Jane, who had arranged the curls earlier, severe distress.

"Why, of course he came!" the maid said, hurrying forward to repair the damage Frederica had caused. "Promptly at three o'clock he presented himself, just like your mama said!"

Frederica looked wildly toward the clock and said, her eyes accusing, "Jane, does that clock work?"

Her puzzled maid, following her glance, nodded.

"It's nearly four o'clock!" Frederica cried. "I thought . . . I thought . . ."

Thinking she understood what her mistress thought, Jane patted Frederica's shoulder in consolation. "Now, my lady," she said, "surely you knew he would come! A man in love—"

"I knew no such thing!" Frederica snapped, rising and taking a turn about the room before returning to her maid's soothing ministrations. "And if you think for one moment that Chilesworth is in love—" She caught herself up on the words and sniffed. "Well, with himself, perhaps! But as for . . ."

"My lady!" the maid gasped.

Seeing her shocked face, Frederica finished with a lame muttering that she just had not thought he would come. Jane's smile was knowing.

"That's the way it always is," the maid said. "A woman in love worries! But you can see he *has* come, and now he awaits you below." She gave a great, gusty, romantic sigh. "Looking like a prince in a fairy tale, too."

Frederica wanted to shout that her intended more closely resembled a toad, but thought better of the words and allowed the maid to help her rearrange her mother's soft silk shawl, shot through with gold, around her shoulders. Squaring those same shoulders, Frederica, head held high, swept down the stairs to the library.

Frederica nodded at Higgins, who threw open the doors with great ceremony. Inside was her father, standing by his desk, looking down at Viscount Chilesworth with concern. Anthony sat, one hand supporting his head as he gazed in abstraction at the fire. A coffee cup was near his right hand, and George was in the process of filling it as Frederica entered. Her brother, straightening, encountered the fire in her eyes and gave a slight warning cough. Both the other men in the room turned toward her.

"Oh! Frederica!" Her father hastened forward to take her hand and, pulling it through the crook of his arm, led her forward until they both stood before Chilesworth, who had risen belatedly, one hand going up to push his hair from his forehead, the other making a quick check of his cravat. "See who has come to see you!"

It was an awkward moment, and Frederica, displeased with each of the men in the room for putting her in this trying position, was determined not to make it any less awkward by anything she might say. Raising an eyebrow, she glanced from her father to George to the viscount and back to her father again.

"Frederica," Chilesworth said, his tone noncommittal.

"Viscount Chilesworth," she returned, her tone the same.

George and the earl exchanged glances. Clearing his throat, the earl said, "Yes, well . . ." He cleared his throat again. "Anthony has something he wishes to ask you, my dear, and George and I are quite *de trop*."

"George," Frederica said with her sweetest smile, so at odds with the daggers in her eyes, "is always *de trop*." Her brother grinned.

"Cut line, Freddie," George said, drawing her wrath at the use of her childhood name. "Everyone here has known you far too long to be taken in by that toplofty manner." He was looking pointedly at Anthony, but the viscount seemed not to receive his message. It was apparent Frederica did, however, and she glared at him.

"Now, now," the earl intervened, motioning his son toward the door. "Deuced awkward situation, but there— least said, soonest mended. Best to go lightly over hard ground, hey, Anthony?"

Viscount Chilesworth, who would have given a great deal to be riding over hard ground at that moment, muttered something about it being better not to go at all. Frederica snorted and cast him such a withering look that the viscount began to wonder if Brazil would be quite as bad as he'd imagined.

"Yes, well," the earl said from the door, "we'll just leave you two to talk."

Forkham pushed his heir through the open doorway and followed. In his hurry, the door shut behind him with a snap. On the other side, he pulled his handkerchief from his pocket and wiped his forehead for several moments as George, his face anxious, watched.

"Father—" George began. The earl shook his head.

"Yes, yes," Forkham said. "I know. But we have to

hope . . . perhaps . . . well! We have to do something, don't we?"

George nodded. "But marriage . . . Freddie and Anthony . . . they look more likely to strangle each other!"

The earl shook his head again. "It's a long shot, George. I do not deny it's a long shot. But Sebastian and I have great hopes that if our children don't kill each other first, they very well may be the making of each other!"

George's face was grave, and it was apparent he remained unconvinced. His father sighed. "Well, if nothing else," the earl suggested, "your sister may be so busy quarreling with Anthony for a while that she will stay out of all the other scrapes she has been forever falling into!"

George was unconvinced of that, too, but having no other plan to offer, he followed his father down the hall to the small sitting room, where the countess sat waiting for them. George's ears, however, remained tuned for any sound of flying books or shattering glass that soon might be emanating from the library.

There was silence for several moments after the earl and George left Frederica Farthingham and Viscount Chilesworth alone together. Anthony, standing by the fireplace, watched covertly as his companion moved to the other side of the room, picking up this object and that, looking at everything but him. Realizing this could go on indefinitely the viscount gave a slight cough. When that did not draw Freddie's attention, he sighed.

"You know, Frederica . . ." Chilesworth started, then wished he'd kept quiet. The sound of his voice seemed to unleash a torrent within her.

"You!" Frederica said, eyes flashing as she picked up a book. For a moment he thought she might heave it at him, as she'd heaved several things when they were children. He prepared to duck, knowing she had a good arm, but

Frederica seemed to collect herself, and he breathed a sigh of relief as she placed the book back on the table.

"*You!*"

The word was said with such loathing that the viscount, who had culled his brain on the way over that afternoon for what he was to say, found the words coming much more readily than he'd expected. "Well, this isn't my idea, either, you know!" he snapped. "So don't think you're the only one being put upon here!"

"Hmmph!" Frederica's nose was in the air and she gave her head a decided shake, causing the curls gathered there to bounce in an attractive way Chilesworth found distracting. It was one of the most annoying things about Frederica since she had grown up, he thought—she was always distracting him. "Of all the—the—" She could not think of a *the* cutting enough, and ended with another "Hmmph!"

The viscount ran his fingers through his hair. "Now see here, Frederica—" he began. She hmmphed once more.

"I told them you would not come," Frederica said. "I thought that even *you* were not such a—a—" She searched her brain for one of the most cutting things she had ever heard George say about anyone and came up with "a curst rum touch as to come—"

"Now just a moment!" Anthony's jaw worked, and his eyes were bright with indignation. One hand went up to disarrange the hair he had tried to bring into order at her entrance. "Here I've come to offer you marriage and you're calling me a curst rum touch, which is not, give me leave to inform you, the phrase I would expect to hear on the tongue of a well-bred young lady, and one I *certainly* do not care to hear from my soon-to-be affianced wife!"

"Well, I will *not* give you leave to inform me!" Frederica said huffily. "And I told you several years ago, Anthony Chilesworth, that I do not believe you are in the position to tell me or anyone else how to go on as a well-bred young lady! And as for being your affianced wife—*ha!*"

Frederica snapped her fingers at him, hoping the action would cover her earlier slip, but she could see by his face that it had not. She'd wished as soon as she'd said the words that they could be unsaid, for she had made up her mind that no matter *what* she referred to this afternoon, it would not be to *the* event that had occurred in what she liked to dismiss as the ancient past. She was doubly sorry the reference had slipped out as she saw Anthony's brow darken further. He fairly purred, "Still playing with hardened rakes, are you, Frederica? I believe I heard something about that. Which is, no doubt, what has led us to this *delightful* tête-à-tête this afternoon!"

Frederica bit her lip as the shot went home, then rallied with, "*Oh*, is that why you're here, Anthony? Now *I* supposed it was because of *your* playing—with rakes and otherwise! Going through a fortune, aren't you, Anthony? Or has your father sent you here because of that proclivity you have for opera dancers and other ladybirds—"

"And what do you know of opera dancers and ladybirds, Frederica?" the viscount demanded. He used such righteous tones that Frederica's anger was further inflamed as he continued. "And I think you should know that if this is the way you usually converse with your gentlemen—or female—acquaintances, I can see how you've garnered what would appear to be a very well-deserved reputation for being fast—"

"How *dare* you?" Frederica sputtered. "*You*, to call *me* fast? Of all the—the—*oh*!" She flounced across the room and threw herself into a chair. Gripping the arms, she said, through teeth that were clamped tight together, "Let me tell you, Viscount Chilesworth, that I would not marry you if you were the last man in this country!"

"And let me tell *you*, Frederica Farthingham, that I would not *ask* you to marry me if you were the last woman on the earth!"

His words, like hers, were said to wither, but his, at least, had the opposite effect. Frederica, instead of appearing insulted, brightened. A smile started to grow on her generous lips as she rose and came toward him, saying, her eyes hopeful, "Wouldn't you, Anthony? Wouldn't you really?"

Frowning at this sudden change in mood, the viscount assured her he would not.

"By all that's wonderful!" Freddie crowed, further astounding him. She took his large, unresisting hand and squeezed it tightly between her own small ones. "Thank you! Oh, thank you, dear Anthony! I take back every— well, almost every—bad thing I have ever said about you! And good day to you! To you, Viscount Chilesworth, a very good day!"

Chapter Six

FREDERICA WAS ALMOST to the door when a bemused Chilesworth, feeling as if his feet had been knocked from under him, stopped her with an irritated "And just where do you think you're going?"

The lady turned a surprised face toward him. "Why, to my room, of course!" she said. "I don't think we have any more to say to each other, do we?"

"Well, of course we do!" The viscount ran his fingers through his hair and wondered when Frederica had become such an infuriating young woman. As a child he had liked her well enough; in fact, he had liked her a great deal. She was game as a pebble for a girl, and not one to pout or put on airs. And when she had made her debut her first season, she'd looked so fragile, so in need of protection, who would have thought that pretty little head could hold the sharp-edged tongue of a shrew.

Visions of Frederica the child vanished as Chilesworth glared at the woman who had taken her place. "I have to say, will you marry me?"

The smile that a moment before had wreathed her face vanished, and Frederica stared at him in shock. To the viscount's horror two large tears gathered in her violet eyes and rolled down her cheeks. She staggered to a nearby chair and sank into it.

"Oh, Anthony!" she said, her lower lip trembling as she rubbed at her eyes. "How *could* you?"

It was such a heartfelt accusation that he could only goggle at her for several moments before it became clear that she was in need of assistance.

"Here," he said, pulling a square of white linen from his pocket. "You never did have a handkerchief about you when you needed it."

Frederica took the snowy linen and made dainty swipes at her eyes as she turned her head away from him. "I thought better of you," she mourned.

Chilesworth stared at her. "Thought . . . better?" he repeated.

"How *could* you ask me to marry you?"

How could I not? the viscount thought, recalling his recent uncomfortable interview with his father. Aloud, in a bracing manner he hoped would put an end to her tears, he said, "Well, you don't have to accept! For goodness sake, Frederica—I've done my part by asking you. Now you do your part by refusing me!"

"But I can't!" the lady wailed, handing back his handkerchief. He stuffed it into a pocket as he demanded with great irritation to know why not.

"Because . . ." she began. "Because Papa says—"

She stopped and glared up at him. "I think it very bad of you to offer for me, Anthony, when not two minutes ago you said you wouldn't ask me to marry you if I were the last woman left on earth!"

"Well, you said you wouldn't marry me if I were the last man in the country," he countered, "and you said what you said before I said what I said. So just tell me we will not suit each other and I'll be on my way."

"Of course we will not suit!" Frederica snapped. "Marry *you*? I'd rather marry a monkey."

"Well, *I'd* rather marry a—a—a *potato* than—"

He was stopped by a sudden giggle that reminded him of his childhood friend, the one who had disappeared Frederica's first season out, when he'd assumed he could dictate to the young woman who'd taken the town by storm much as he'd dictated to the little girl she'd once been.

"Oh, Anthony, really!" Frederica scoffed. "A potato!"

In spite of himself, an answering grin dawned on the viscount's face. "Couldn't think of anything quick," he excused himself.

Handsomely Frederica conceded that she already had taken the best comparison before he had a chance. Then she returned to the point.

"Come now, Anthony!" she coaxed. "Couldn't you just tell your father that you thought better of making me an offer?"

"I could," the viscount answered, "but I won't."

Frederica frowned at him. "And why not?"

He did not respond at once, asking instead if she couldn't tell *her* father that she had changed her mind and could not bring herself to the sticking point when the viscount proposed.

"No" was the bald reply.

"Why not?"

"Bath," Frederica said.

Chilesworth shook his head and gave it a slight tap with the ball of his hand. "Must not have heard right," he apologized. "Did you say Bath?"

Frederica nodded.

"You don't want to . . . take one?" The question was cautious. She frowned at him.

"Don't be an idiot, Anthony!" she told him. "I don't want to go there!"

"Oh." He digested that. "You know, Frederica," he said, "it is not considered good manners to be calling someone an idiot."

"Well, it is not good manners to be one!" Frederica responded. "And please remember, you are not the one to instruct me in polite behavior. Don't want to take a bath, indeed! What a sap-skull!"

"*Sap-skull?*" The viscount frowned at her. "It is no more flattering than *idiot*, Freddie, and I like it even less! You'd do a great deal better if you'd learn to mind that runaway tongue of yours, let me tell you!"

"My name is Frederica! And what I learn to mind or don't learn to mind is of no interest to you!"

"It will be if we are engaged."

"We are not going to *be* engaged!"

"Then refuse my offer."

"*I can't!*" Frederica was much exasperated. "I *told* you that!" She gave him the cajoling gaze that never failed to win her what she wanted from any number of admirers. "Withdraw it, instead!"

He shook his head and sighed. "Cut line, Freddie," he ordered, "and tell me about Bath."

She frowned. "Frederica. And there will be no need to tell you about Bath if you simply withdraw your offer."

"Can't." The word was brief.

Her frown grew. "Why not?"

"Brazil."

Now it was Frederica's turn to shake her head, and she did, tilting it to one side as she surveyed him in puzzlement. "I . . . beg your pardon?"

"Brazil," he said. "I'm not going there."

"Well, I don't blame you," Frederica said. "But what Brazil has to do with—"

The viscount sighed. "My father," he said, "is not best pleased with me at the moment." He ignored a pious "I can see why" and continued. "He says that my . . . ah, excesses are such that if I do not mend my ways, he will ship me off to my uncle in Brazil to see if Uncle Edward can bring about a change in me."

"Hmmph!" It occurred to the viscount that Frederica Farthingham had a most grating way of sniffing "Hmmph!"—and he frowned at her.

"I don't see that that's such a terrible threat!" Frederica said. "I mean, you're a man grown. What's your father going to do if you refuse to go, shanghai you?"

A look at the viscount's grim face made it apparent that such a threat had been issued, and Frederica's eyes widened in surprise. "You don't mean—" she began.

"My father," the viscount said, his tone very, very dry, "assures me that he could survive without my embarrassing—and expensive—presence for some time. _And_ he tells me—subtly, of course—that he knows people who would be willing to relieve him of said embarrassing presence, if necessary." Chilesworth ran a hand through his hair and his face grew pensive. "While I believe I could account quite well for myself in a fight, should anyone try to shanghai me, I find that I do not want it to come to that. I do not really wish to be estranged from my father."

Frederica sniffed again, ignoring the last part of his speech. "You _are_ a wild one, Anthony," she reminded him.

"Oh-ho!" the viscount retorted, with what she considered a deplorable lack of tact. "And you, of course, are in a position to judge that!"

Frederica reddened as she took a turn about the room. She stopped by his side a few moments later to suggest in her most hopeful voice that he might _like_ Brazil.

The viscount's snort was on a par with Frederica's sniff. "My _uncle_," he told her, "is a _missionary_ there."

"Oh." Frederica digested that bit of information.

"He does numerous good works."

"Oh." The picture grew bleaker.

"I do not intend to be one of them."

In great discouragement Frederica sank into a chair. "It is too bad of you," she said.

The viscount agreed and studied her bent head. "Now cut line, Freddie, and tell me about Bath."

"Frederica," she corrected, then added, "Great-aunt Honoria." The viscount thought for a moment.

"Your Great-aunt Honoria?"

Frederica's head moved up and down.

"I thought she died years ago!"

Now her head moved side to side.

"Lives in Bath, does she?"

"Yes." Frederica picked up a paperweight from her father's desk, then put it down again.

"What's that got to do with you?"

Frederica raised troubled eyes to his. "Father says if I don't accept your proposal, I must go live with her. In Bath."

"Oh." The viscount tried for a bracing tone. "Nice town, Bath."

Frederica eyed him cynically. "My Aunt Honoria," she said, "keeps cats."

"Nice animals, cats."

"Forty-seven of them, at last count."

"The more, the merrier."

"She also has a hideous little dog named Pugsley."

"Always liked dogs, myself."

Frederica's gaze was frosty. "Perhaps you would like to go live with Aunt Honoria," she suggested, her polite accents so at odds with her dagger-darting eyes that he grinned.

"And perhaps you would like to go be saved in Brazil."

Frederica's head moved from left to right several times, as if in slow cadence to a dirge only she could hear. "I wish I were dead," she said.

A gallant Viscount Chilesworth refrained from saying that he rather wished so, too.

Frederica eyed him. "Or, I wish *you* were dead . . ."

"Almost anything to oblige, Freddie," he replied, his tone cheerful, "but not that!"

"Frederica!" There was silence for several moments before she continued.

"I wish I'd taken one of my other offers." She was staring into the fire as he said with real sincerity that he wished she had, too. It was apparent he felt extremely ill-used as he asked why she had not.

"Because I did not wish to marry any of them!" she responded, glaring up at him. "I have never thought—I do not think—" She lifted her chin and said that she was not at all sure that marriage would suit her.

"Well, I'm *very* sure it won't suit me!" the viscount told her. "Not marriage to anybody! But this! Marriage to *you*! I'd as lief be tied to a leopard as to a spitfire such as you—"

Frederica wished aloud, in oh so polite tones, that the former could be arranged.

The viscount rolled his eyes and said with a loftiness that made her yearn to slap him that such talk was getting them nowhere. Frederica continued to frown, abstracted, for several moments as she surveyed him. Suddenly she straightened. Chilesworth could tell an idea was forming in her mind, and he eyed her with foreboding as she rose and paced several times around the chair before shouting "That's it!" in a triumphant voice that made him jump.

"For goodness sake, Freddie!" He was irritated. "What are you about, 'that's-itting!' a fellow when he's trying to think?"

"Don't call me Freddie!" she told him. "How many times must I tell you that? Frederica! My name is Frederica! And what you'd use to think with, I don't know! Besides, you needn't try, because I've got a plan!"

"I'm sure!" the viscount said, scoffing. "Is this a plan like the plan to race Baron Barnsley to Brighton—that wonderful plan that landed you in this mess?" The way her eyes widened made it apparent she'd hoped he hadn't known the full extent of her latest indiscretion, and he nodded, satisfied.

"Oh, yes!" he assured her, "I know about that. It was all over town before the cat could lick its ear. And even if I weren't one of the first to hear gossip in London—which I am, you know—my father assures me *your* father considers the bad baron the straw that broke the already loaded camel's back!"

She had reddened and was avoiding his eyes as the viscount continued with great sarcasm, "Or perhaps your plan is like the plan to fly off the roof you had when we were children and which ended in your broken collarbone? Or is this a plan like the plan—"

In disgust Frederica thought that there was a great deal to be said for not knowing people as an adult whom you knew in your childhood. Especially if those people have long, odious memories like Anthony's.

Roundly she told him that if he was going to be that way, she'd tell her father he hadn't offered for her at all and he could just take his lumps—and his trip to Brazil. The viscount, who believed her capable of just such an act when in a temper—and it seemed to him Freddie was almost always in a temper since she'd grown up—narrowed his eyes but kept silent.

"Now listen, Anthony," she said, "as I understand it, we're both in disgrace with our parents at present. You with more cause than I, I might add, because you've done any number of gossip-inspiring things lately, like taking snuff from Lady Bentley's wrist and being challenged to a duel by her oh so jealous husband, and betting you could race a goose blindfolded through Hyde Park, and firing off your pistol to quaff a candle at Watiers while all I did was, well . . ."

The viscount gave a repressive frown and agreed they were both in disgrace.

"And both our fathers believe that marriage will be the making of us, am I right?"

The viscount said that she was.

"They think it will settle us down."

"Yes." The viscount gave a glum nod. "They do. And why they think that, when they have only to look at you to know you are the most unsettling—"

"Oh, yes!" Frederica rose. "Talk about *me*! When *you*—"

A soft tap at the door was followed a moment later by the appearance of the Earl of Forkham. His expression was one of anxious inquiry as he stood surveying them.

"Is everything all right in here?" the earl questioned, giving both their faces close consideration as he gazed about the room for signs of thrown books or broken glass. Frederica smiled at him.

"Everything is just fine, Father," she said.

"It *is?*" both men echoed. The earl looked at her with suspicion when he realized his words also had come from Viscount Chilesworth's mouth.

"Of course," Frederica said, giving the viscount a surreptitious pinch and ignoring his indignant "*Ouch!*"

"Then, your business together is concluded?" her father asked, opening the door farther. Behind him stood her mother and George; at sight of them Frederica smiled.

"Almost," she told them, her voice gay. "Do come in! Do! Anthony has asked me to marry him and I am about to give him my reply."

"Oh, Lord," muttered Anthony and George together, then exchanged commiserating glances as the earl and his lady held their breath.

"Well?" four voices chorused when they could no longer bear the suspense. Frederica stood, the center of attention, pleased now that she had worn her rose silk gown, which fell from its high waist to several rows of ruffles at the hem. She touched one of the small puffed sleeves and gathered her mother's shawl more closely about her as she smiled at them all. One did, after all, like to be well dressed when all eyes were upon one.

"Yes, dear Anthony," she cooed. "Yes. Yes. Yes."

Chapter
Seven

IT WAS FREDERICA and George who noticed Viscount Chilesworth did not appear as overjoyed as was usually expected of a young man who had just asked a young woman to marry him and had her say yes. In fact, George, watching with a critical eye, could not help but think that his friend stood as if stuffed; the viscount's eyes were glassy, his skin pale, and the muscles in his jaw bulged. He looked, George decided, remarkably unwell.

The Earl and Countess of Forkham did not choose to notice Anthony's less than enthusiastic response. Both were much too relieved to hear Frederica say yes to pay attention to anyone else's emotions. "My dear!" Lucinda trilled, coming forward to hug her daughter. The countess gave her less than comfortable child one, two, then three fond squeezes before turning to her future son-in-law.

"Anthony!" Lucinda threw her arms around the viscount and gazed tearfully up into his harassed face. "You'll never know how happy this makes me!"

"You'll never know how happy it makes me, either." The viscount's words were strangled, and George had to bite his tongue to keep from laughing. Even Frederica smiled.

"Well, well!" The earl was in hearty humor. First he

shook his daughter's hand, then that of his future son-in-law. He shook George's hand, too, and swept his wife off the floor in a huge embrace. "This calls for a celebration!"

Shouting for Higgins to bring wine, the earl drew his wife, who had started off to hug their daughter yet again, into his arms and gave her a happy kiss on the cheek. With a wink he told the viscount that if that young man wished to kiss his affianced wife, they would all understand—this once.

A stone-faced Anthony deliberated between doing as was suggested and informing them all that he would rather kiss a viper. Deciding that in this instance, at least, discretion was the better part of valor, the viscount moved forward to salute Frederica's cheek. His lips barely brushed her skin, and as they passed her ear he whispered, "Of all the—" in a tone that did not bode well for his intended.

"We must talk!" Frederica hissed back, one hand catching his lapel in a manner her parents might consider tender if they wished but which Anthony found held unsuspected meaning when he tried to pull away. Seeing George watching them closely, Frederica fixed a big smile on her lips as she gazed up at the viscount.

"Yes," Chilesworth assured her, his voice almost as grim as it was low. "We must."

"George," Frederica called, ignoring Chilesworth's words as she smiled up at her new fiancé as if he were her heart's delight, "aren't you going to congratulate us?"

Her brother came forward to shake the viscount's hand, then held his sister by the shoulders as he gazed down at her, trying as he often did to probe what lay behind her eyes. "Should I, Freddie?" he asked, one eyebrow raised.

"Frederica," she replied automatically. Her look was one of innocence. "And I don't know what you mean."

"Don't you, my dear?" George's tone and smile were quizzical, and Frederica felt the color rising in her cheeks. Turning away, she grabbed Chilesworth's arm and tugged him toward the farthest corner of the room, saying loudly that there was something she wanted him to see there.

"What?" The question was curt as Anthony glanced with distaste at the heavy tomes on the shelves in front of him. He hoped that on top of everything else that had happened to him that day he wasn't about to discover his future bride was a blasted bluestocking. A distracted glance around the room informed him that the earl and his wife were watching him and Frederica in delight, and Chilesworth's frown grew.

"Anything!" Frederica said, her voice urgent but low, to keep it from reaching her parents' ears. "Pretend you're interested in anything you see! Do I have to do it all myself?" The viscount looked down at her in surprise, and Frederica restrained an impulse to slap him. Inside she wanted to scream as she hissed, "It's a ruse, you idiot! I needed to talk with you alone, so I said there was something I wanted you to see here!"

"Oh!" Obligingly the viscount lifted a book at random from the shelf and gazed uncomprehendingly at it as he tried once again to convince his betrothed that it was not becoming to call one's future husband an idiot. Frederica ignored him as she began to speak.

"For goodness sake, Anthony, buck up!" the lady said, smiling up at him for her family's benefit. It occurred to the viscount that her words were coming through gritted teeth, and there was a dangerous spark in her eyes. "You can spare me this lecture, because I have no intention of being your future bride. Don't worry. And don't say anything to anyone until we have an opportunity to talk, in private. We can do so tonight, at Almack's—my mother and I are engaged to go. Be there."

"Almack's?" Chilesworth repeated. It occurred to him that that might not be the best place to be private, and his tone made it apparent that the thought of putting in an appearance at the marriage mart appalled him. He said the word so loudly that Frederica was forced to smile even as she longed to kick him in the shins.

"What's that about Almack's, dear?" Frederica's mother questioned as she came forward. She was followed by George, who took the book Anthony was holding and gave it a close inspection.

"I didn't know you were interested in Greek, Anthony," George said, his surprise obvious.

"Oh, yes." The viscount gave a careless nod. "Been interested in it these past ten years."

"I see." George's tone was bland. "And you can read it upside down, too."

"What?" A startled Chilesworth turned red as his friend explained Anthony had been holding the book upside down. Thoughtfully George replaced the book on the shelf, and Frederica, glaring at her betrothed, said, "I was just telling Anthony that we are bound to Almack's tonight, Mother."

The countess, glancing from one to the other of them, said in placating tones that they needn't go tonight; now that they had something to celebrate, perhaps dear Anthony might like to join them for a family coze. And his parents! Of course, his parents must be invited too!

Frederica stared at her in horror.

"But we *must* go to Almack's!" Frederica said. "We *must*! I quite have my heart *set* on it!"

"Frederica, really," the countess protested, smiling at Chilesworth in such a way as to say she really didn't know what had come over her daughter. "I'm sure if dear Anthony does not wish to go to Almack's, we needn't do so tonight."

"Of course we needn't," seconded the earl. "Shabby sort of place, anyway! Always thought so! Lemonade and orgeat!" He gave a visible shudder.

A frowning Chilesworth, who was trying to decipher the rolling of Frederica's expressive eyes and the head shruggings his future wife was using to communicate with him, interrupted to say that if Frederica had her heart set on going, then they all of course must go.

"Whatever Frederica wants," Chilesworth said, his warm words at odds with his cold voice. His fiancée smiled.

"Thank you, Anthony," she said. The words were honeyed and the viscount had to fight down the most unchivalrous wish that she might choke on them.

"Of course." He bowed over her hand. "Until tonight . . . Frederica."

Only George and Frederica heard the warning behind the words, and it was a thoughtful George who saw his friend to the door.

"Is everything all right, old man?" George asked as the viscount received his hat and cane from the ever-correct Higgins.

Chilesworth's smile was tight. "I'm to marry your sister, George," he said. "You must congratulate me. What could be more right than that?"

George, who could think of many things, put a bracing hand on his friend's shoulder and said, "I wish you much luck, Anthony."

Cramming his hat on his head as he exited through the door the butler held open for him, Chilesworth thought grimly that he was sure to need it.

It wanted only three minutes to eleven when Viscount Chilesworth strolled through the doors of Almack's that evening. Frederica, who had been watching for him since her own arrival at ten P.M., was ready to scream. Several times she had decided he wasn't coming, so one might have assumed that the sight of him in correct ball dress, his linen immaculate, his well-made black coat cut to fit tightly over his powerful shoulders, would have filled her with relief.

One would have been wrong.

Frederica had delayed her own arrival until ten P.M. because she hoped to find the viscount at Almack's ahead of her. She had planned to make an entrance that would, while not changing Chilesworth's adamant aversion to marriage, at least let him know what he was missing by her fervent desire not to be his wife.

She was looking particularly fetching in her gown of high-waisted blue silk, which circled the tops of her full breasts. The soft skirt caressed her ankles when she walked. A dainty dark blue ribbon, shot through with gold, was tied at the high waist and edged the sleeves and neckline.

Frederica had spent much time on her toilette that evening, directing Jane to dress her hair at least three different ways before they achieved one on which they both agreed. She had tried on and discarded various pieces of jewelry, finally settling on the intricate gold necklace with the small blue flowers of sapphires that, when she moved, seemed to dance just above the hollow between her breasts. Sapphire eardrops, also shaped to resemble tiny flowers, and a flower sapphire comb in her hair completed the effect. Frederica's father had bought her the jewels for her recent birthday, and Frederica had the satisfaction of knowing from the envious glances cast her way that tomorrow the considerable number of young ladies who always followed the Lady Frederica's fashion lead would begin frantic searches through the leading jewelry shops in London looking for similar pieces.

The countess had visited her daughter's room several times while Frederica was dressing, adjuring the younger woman to hurry so that they would not keep dear Anthony waiting.

Frederica, who wanted to snap her fingers and say Anthony could wait forever, curbed her tongue and turned red with the effort of keeping the words unsaid. Misunderstanding, the countess exchanged knowing looks with Jane and laughed. "Ah, my dear, you are nervous!"

A sapphire eardrop slipped through Frederica's fingers,

and she turned anxious eyes toward her mother. How could she *know*?

The countess smiled. "And you want to look your best for Anthony!"

Frederica relaxed and bobbed her head in apparent confusion. Better for her mother to think *that*, than to wonder what was really causing her daughter's stomach to vibrate with butterfly wings. The countess was right— Frederica *was* nervous, but for reasons other than her mother might think. As she prepared for her next encounter with Chilesworth, Frederica's biggest fear was that the viscount wouldn't agree to her scheme, and then they *would* find themselves in the basket.

Her fear had grown during the past hour as Frederica again and again searched the doorway in vain for sight of the viscount's tall frame, peering over various dance partners' shoulders and peeping in that certain way above her flirtatious fan. Before she, her mother, and her father had left home, they'd seen George leaving for Cribb's Parlor, and Frederica couldn't help but wonder.

"Well, really, George!" her mother had scolded at sight of her son. "The night of your sister's engagement and you choose Cribb's Parlor over accompanying the family to Almack's?"

A grinning George kissed the countess and his sister lightly on the cheek and with a cheerful "It isn't *my* engagement!" left them, after letting fall that Anthony had been engaged with the same party George was attending. For the last half hour Frederica had entertained the terrible fear that her betrothed had refused her summons and taken himself off to what she was sure was a hideous, low-life place that, in her present mood, she considered far too good for either her future husband or her brother. So Frederica was not in the best of moods when Chilesworth at last made his way across the room to her—which, she noted crossly, he was in no hurry to do, having flirted for ten minutes with

Lady Jersey, and another ten with that insipid Annabella Chittington, who everyone said was a beauty but who Frederica was *sure* squinted.

Frederica caught herself up guiltily on that thought and was giving herself a severe mental chastisement, reminding herself that she had no interest in who Anthony honored with his attentions, and if he was so drawn to ninnies who had no more to say for themselves than "Oh, yes, my lord" and "Oh, no, my lord" and "La! What a wicked one you are, my lord," it was no concern of hers.

Her internal dialogue was interrupted by her betrothed's voice. "I take it," the viscount said as the orchestra struck up a waltz, "that that frown is for me."

Frederica glared up at him but responded, her voice sugary sweet, "Why, Anthony! Is it you? I didn't see you come in. In fact, I'd almost forgotten we were to meet here tonight! So why ever would I be frowning at *you*?"

"I have no idea," the viscount replied. Glancing around, he noticed that several members of his mother's generation were regarding them with benign smiles and talking behind their fans.

"Botheration!" he said.

"What?" Frederica looked at him in surprise, and he took her hand abruptly. "Dance with me, Freddie."

"Frederica," she said, bristling at the command in his voice. "And I will not! For your information I am engaged to dance with . . ." She consulted her dance card and directed a dazzling smile toward the painfully shy young man who stood two feet away, deliberating as to whether he should approach her while she and Viscount Chilesworth were frowning so fiercely at each other. "My dear Mr. Mattington here."

At her welcoming smile Mr. Mattington screwed up his courage and came forward, bowing with great nervousness over her hand.

"Mattington, eh?" The viscount said the other gentle-

man's name quite pleasantly and dropped a heavy hand on
his shoulder. Young Mr. Mattington gulped. "I'm sure
Mattington won't mind giving up his dance to one of your
oldest friends."

Mr. Mattington did mind. He minded very much. Ever
since he had arrived in London two weeks earlier and had
seen Frederica Farthingham laughing in the park, her face
framed by a brimmed hat of cerulean blue, he had known
himself in love with her. He had plotted and plotted to attain
this waltz with the lady tonight, and now . . .

He glanced up into Chilesworth's eyes and gulped again.
While he had seen Frederica Farthingham in the park, he
also had seen the viscount boxing at Jackson's.

"No," Mr. Mattington said, his disconsolation apparent
as he stepped back, his shoulders slumped. "No, of course
not. Unless . . ." He brightened for a moment and looked
hopefully toward Frederica. "Unless you would prefer not
to change partners?"

About to say hotly that she had no intention of giving up
her prescribed partner for this usurper, Frederica looked at
her willing but slender knight and at Anthony, at least a
head taller and more than a few pounds heavier. Reading the
message in the viscount's eyes, which assured her that he
was very close to being done with her games, Frederica
said, with what grace she could muster, "It is very good of
you, Mr. Mattington. The viscount and I are the oldest of
friends, you know. And he is always so insistent about
having his way."

Mr. Mattington did not know, but his nod was humble as
he stepped back another pace. The discouragement in his
eyes prompted Frederica to add in her kindest voice, "But
I do hope we might dance a country dance later this
evening."

Mr. Mattington brightened as the viscount gave a low
chuckle.

"Oh, yes!" Mr. Mattington said. "I will look forward to it."

"I will look forward to it too!" Frederica called over her shoulder as Chilesworth, feeling he had been patient long enough, pulled her into his arms and swept her out into the mass of twirling couples, whose bright clothing and whirling movements put the dazzled Mr. Mattington in mind of the world's most exquisite kaleidoscope.

Chapter
Eight

"SHAME ON YOU!" Frederica scolded as she glared up at her escort, wondering what there was about dancing with this provoking man that made her dizzy as they turned gracefully among the gliding figures. It was ridiculous! He must be doing it wrong. Waltzing never made her dizzy! And why hadn't she noticed before how very tall he was, and so broad-shouldered. It wasn't as if she hadn't seen him in the past three years; as her mother had pointed out earlier, she'd met him everywhere. She'd even danced with him once or twice, when it couldn't be avoided.

Hmmm. Come to think of it, maybe she *had* noticed his shoulders. . . .

Not wanting to think about that, Frederica gave herself a mental shake as the viscount quirked an eyebrow. "Shame on *me*, Freddie?"

"Frederica!" She refused to acknowledge his meaning. "And yes, shame on you! That was *very* badly done! Poor Mr. Mattington!"

The viscount glanced back to where the young man stood, watching them with a dazed expression of great happiness on his face. "Silly cawker," he said indulgently.

"What?"

He glanced down in surprise and realized she'd misunderstood. "Not you, Freddie," he assured her, tightening his grip about her waist. "Young Mattington there."

It hadn't before occurred to the viscount—or he had, perhaps, as a matter of convenience forgotten—that Frederica could be such a satisfying armful, and the realization was doing strange things to his equilibrium.

True, he'd watched her whirling around with this young buck or that at any number of parties, and he'd noticed how her eyes sparkled and her face glowed, and how her partners always seemed to be enjoying themselves immensely. But it was hard for him at those times to think about holding the Lady Frederica when he was much more likely to be warding off blows! Still, he was not warding off blows now—far from it—and his hold tightened again.

Frederica, who found that the tightening at her waist made it even more difficult to breathe, took a ragged breath and said, "What do you mean?"

Chilesworth grinned. "The silly boy is in love with you!"

Frederica stiffened. "Any number of men have not found that idea so ridiculous," she informed him.

The viscount's grin grew. "More pity to them!"

"Well!" Frederica wriggled in his grasp, and Chilesworth's grip grew firmer. After the day he'd had he had no intention of letting an angry Frederica Farthingham stomp from the dance floor and leave him standing there alone. "Of all the arrogant, pompous—*let me go!*"

"Not on your life!" the viscount said, twirling her ever faster in an effort to keep her from breaking away.

"You're holding me much too tight!" she informed him with the censuring tones of his dowager grandmother. He grinned.

"Are you calm enough now to behave rationally if I loosen my grip?" he asked.

A huffy Frederica informed him that she was always rational.

His grin grew. "Yes," he agreed. "That's what got us into this fine mess!"

Her eyes sparked dangerously, but she did not attempt to pull away when she felt a slight loosening of his hold on her waist. "I didn't want you to make a scene," he told her as he slowed his pace, allowing her to catch her breath. "We're being watched."

"What—" Frederica glanced from left to right, her vision largely obscured by those broad shoulders on which she'd tried earlier not to dwell. The viscount nodded his head toward the wall where their mothers sat, their heads together, as several of their boon companions huddled around. All eyes were on the dancing couple, and Frederica groaned. "Drat," she said.

"My sentiments exactly."

"I suppose that rules out all chance of our keeping our 'engagement' a secret."

The viscount's voice was acidic as he said that only a sap-skull would think there had been any chance at all of that.

"Then you certainly should have thought so!" Frederica said, firing up. Chilesworth's eyebrows rose.

"Was that your Grand Plan?" he asked scoffingly. "To keep our engagement a secret?"

Said with such sarcasm, in the midst of always crowded Almack's, Frederica was forced to admit—to herself only—that the stratagem was, perhaps, less than brilliant. She had no intention of admitting as much to Chilesworth, however, and said, her voice loud, "And do you have a better idea?"

The viscount's hand pressed warningly on her waist as her voice rose; belatedly Frederica realized that several of the couples around them were regarding Chilesworth and herself with a great deal of interest. She sighed. "I suppose," she said, "that I shall have to think again."

The viscount's tone was polite as he said she mustn't strain herself, this being the first time she'd ever tried to perform a thinking act. She brought her heel squarely down on his instep.

"Sorry." The word came out sweet at his surprised yelp, and Chilesworth glared down at her.

"You did that on purpose!" he charged.

"Well, *I* can't help it if you can't keep your big feet out from under mine!" she countered.

The viscount ground his teeth, and they twirled in silence for several moments before he said, gazing straight over her head, "Do you know, Frederica, that you are the only thing I know of that can make life with my missionary uncle in Brazil seem almost enchanting?"

"Really?" The hope in her eyes could not be concealed. "Really, Anthony? That's wonderful! I'm sure you will like it there. Lord Brumley returned just last year, and he says the climate is quite salu—salu—"

"Salubrious," the viscount supplied. "Yes, I know. Brumley has told everyone in England about his adventures in Brazil, and how much he enjoyed them. One can only wonder why he returned. Unless—and this is only my theory, you understand—Napoleon has, in his devious way, hired Brumley as an agent for the French in the hopes that the good lord will bore us all to death, and there will be no one left to fight for England when the French land their armada."

"I am sure you will enjoy Brazil just as much," Frederica assured him, ignoring his comments on the long-winded and self-consequential Lord Brumley. The viscount almost stopped dancing.

"Don't be ridiculous!" he said.

Frederica looked at him in confusion. "But you just said—"

"I said *almost* Frederica. *Almost* you make my uncle and Brazil look tempting. I have no intention of going there."

"Oh." She sounded so deflated that he grinned.

"Don't worry, my dear," he told her, his face cheerful.

"I've a race tomorrow in which I may very well break my neck. Then you'll be rid of your unwanted fiancé"

"Yes, I know." Her tone was absent. "I have ten pounds riding on you. But you are such a good driver, Anthony, that we cannot depend on any harm coming to you."

The viscount choked, and she gazed at him questioningly.

"My dear," he said, "the depth of your feeling unmans me!"

Frederica frowned. "Don't be ridiculous, Anthony."

"That you would back me in this—"

Frederica said candidly that she'd made her bet before he made his proposal; otherwise she'd have taken his opponent's side.

"I would not have expected you to back me in anything, Frederica," Chilesworth said, and there was added meaning behind his words. Frederica felt her color rise as she informed him that whatever else he was had never blinded her to the fact that he also was an excellent horseman.

"And that you have such faith in my skill," Chilesworth continued, as if much moved, "even believing that I will not kill myself, so you'd far rather see me in Brazil!"

Frederica's frown grew. "I have never wished you dead, Anthony," she said. The words were as stiff as her backbone. "Certainly I do not wish you that. You used to be well enough, before—"

"Before?" The music had stopped but still he held her hand.

Frederica tried to pull away from him, and when she could not, snapped, "Before you became so odious and overbearing and such an expert on how a young lady should go on in the world!"

"Well, if you'd gone on as I tried to tell you, you wouldn't be in this mess right now, Frederica, so perhaps—"

In unison they became aware that their raised voices had drawn a curious crowd. Frederica was the first to smile.

"Oh, Anthony!" she said, slapping him playfully on the shoulder with her fan. "How you *do* love to tease!"

The viscount smiled, too, a smile that did not reach his eyes. "And how teasable you are, my dear Frederica!" He lifted her hand to his lips and kissed it, then tucked that hand firmly in the crook of his elbow as, bowing and smiling, he led her out of the small group that had surrounded them.

"Is this why you wanted me to come to Almack's?" he asked, low-voiced, as they continued to smile for their interested audience. "So we could quarrel? In public?"

Stung, Frederica said of course not, she had a plan to discuss with him. "And if you weren't so quarrelsome, Anthony, we would have discussed it by now!"

"Me?" The viscount's smile was becoming decidedly fixed, and his teeth were clamped together as he leaned toward her. *"Me? You're* the *shrew—"*

"Shrew?" Frederica jerked her hand from his arm and bristled up at him. "You, sir, are a—a—"

Behind her, a tentative voice sounded. "Is everything all right, Lady Frederica?"

Frederica whirled and leveled such a fierce glance on young Mr. Mattington that he blanched. Instantly her brow cleared.

"Mr. Mattington!" she cried. "Is it time for our dance?"

With one eye on the frowning viscount, Mr. Mattington cleared his throat several times and said that yes, yes, he rather thought it was, although he could be mistaken. . . .

"You are." Chilesworth was curt, reaching for Frederica's hand. The lady whipped it away from him and planted it and her other hand firmly on Mr. Mattington's arm.

"But no!" Frederica purred. "You are not!" She playfully wagged a finger at the younger man. "For a moment I had quite thought you'd forgotten me!"

"Oh, no, Lady Frederica!" Mr. Mattington breathed, adoration glowing in his eyes. "I would never, *never* do that!"

Frederica, who had not seen adoration glowing in any man's eyes for several hours now, began to feel insensibly better.

"Never, Mr. Mattington?" she repeated.

"Never!" came the heartfelt reply.

A pleased Frederica turned an imperious nose toward the viscount. "You will excuse us, Chilesworth," she said with a sniff.

"Dashed if I will—" the viscount began, then turned angrily at a tap on his shoulder. His anger turned to stuttering shock as he said, "*S-s-sir!*"

The viscount's father's smile was silky as he gazed at his son. "A word with you, Anthony," said the earl.

"B-but I am trying to talk to Frederica," the viscount said, stammering. The Earl of Manningham turned a charming smile in her direction.

"You are looking as lovely as ever, Frederica," the earl said, bowing and raising the startled lady's hand to his lips. Frederica blushed.

"My . . . my lord!" she said. Frederica saw that behind Anthony's father was her own, and she bit her lip.

"And I would like a word with *you*, Frederica," her own father said. There was a look in his eye that boded her ill, and she gripped Mr. Mattington's arm tighter.

"Of course, Papa," she said. "As soon as I am free! Mr. Mattington here—"

"Will excuse us, I am sure," Forkham finished for her, favoring the young man with just the right smile of condescension. "A family matter, you know."

Mr. Mattington's face fell. "Of course," he said. The earl almost felt sorry for him.

"Find yourself another young lady to dance with," Forkham suggested.

Mr. Mattington sighed. "It would not be the same," the young man said mournfully.

"That's for sure!" Chilesworth snorted. Frederica flashed him a now-you've-done-it look as the viscount's father gazed from one to the other of them and back again.

"Most loverlike," Manningham commented.

Anthony flushed.

"My lord," Frederica said desperately, "if Anthony and I might have just a word . . ."

The fathers exchanged glances and Manningham shrugged. "Why not?" he questioned. Frederica's father had no objection, and she grabbed the viscount's arm.

"Now look what you've done," Chilesworth muttered as they withdrew a few feet.

"Now look what we've *both* done!" Frederica corrected him, keeping an eye on the determined-looking gentlemen off to her right. "And listen! I have no more desire to wed you than you have to wed me, Anthony, but I said we were to be wed in front of my family to give us time."

"Time?" the viscount repeated.

She nodded. "If we pretend to be engaged, it will give me time to look about for a . . . more suitable mate."

The viscount goggled at her. "While you're engaged to *me*?" He snorted. "I think not!"

Frederica turned her back to her father and Manningham and glared up at her betrothed. "My father wants me to marry. So much so that he has countenanced this engagement to *you*!" Her tone made it plain how desperate she considered her father to be.

"Your father," Chilesworth informed her at his most blighting, "wants you to settle down and behave like a lady."

"Yes, well . . ." Behind her, Frederica could feel Forkham's and Manningham's growing impatience. She said, the words coming in haste, "That is why we must play for time. Because it will give both of us an opportunity to mend our ways and provide passage out of this mess. Don't you see?"

Chilesworth, who took the glum position that there *was* no way out, had no better plan to offer and kept silent. Frederica gazed anxiously up at him.

"We must pretend to be engaged at least until we have time to talk further," she said. "I will tell my father we've had a lover's spat."

"A *what*?"

"A lover's spat," she repeated, frowning at him. "And you will tell your father the same thing."

"As if they'd believe that, when we have both been at pains today to make it clear to them that we are far from enamored of each other!"

"We will tell them we find we were mistaken in our affections—or lack of affections," Frederica said, thinking rapidly. Her voice and demeanor were so calm that the viscount could do little more than goggle at her and try to remember if insanity ran in his friend George's family. "We will tell them that we actually have been very much attracted to each other for years, but we both fought our feelings because of a silly quarrel we had several years ago—they know something happened then but not what— and because we thought the other did not care. We will tell them that tonight, while dancing, we revealed our true feelings to each other, then had a falling-out."

Chilesworth, who was gazing at her in wonder that bordered on alarm, opened and closed his mouth several times before asking, one eyebrow raised, "And what did we quarrel about, dearest?"

Frederica sniffed. "I did not like the way you looked at Annabella Chittington."

The viscount grinned. "Why, Freddie! I didn't know you noticed!"

"Frederica!" she snapped. "And you"—she sniffed

again—"felt I was paying undue attention to young Mr. Mattington, there."

"That puppy!" The viscount was revolted. "As if I would ever be jealous of such a young—"

Frederica gave his arm a warning pinch as she heard her father move restlessly behind her. "Love does strange things to people, Anthony!" she said. "Remember that! And do not give us away until we have an opportunity to speak further. I see now that trying to talk with you at Almack's was not the best idea—"

"Well, I could have told you that!" the viscount responded. "Of all the foolish meeting places—"

Frederica pinched his arm once more before turning and offering a smiling face to her father. "Now then, Papa," she said. "You wanted to speak with me?"

Chapter Nine

YES, FREDERICA FOUND, her father did want to speak with her. He had, in fact, a great deal to say. He and Manningham, he informed her, could not help but notice that as quickly as their wives gave news of the betrothal to the world—just to fifteen or twenty of their most trusted confidants, you understand, and told in the strictest confidence—so did the betrothed couple give lie to their words.

Frederica, trying to listen with half an ear while she watched with anxiety the faces of Chilesworth and Manningham, who were standing just beyond earshot several feet away (for she never could depend on what such an unpredictable young man as Anthony might say or do while on his high ropes), had to be recalled to their conversation by her father several times.

"Well, Frederica?" the earl said.

There was no answer, and Forkham's face darkened. "Well, Frederica?" he repeated.

The lady started. "It was a lover's spat," she said automatically.

Her father shook his head. "I beg your pardon?"

"It was a lover's spat, Father," she said. "That was why Anthony and I were quarreling."

Her father stared at her. "Frederica," he said, "you haven't heard a word I've said to you, have you?"

Noticing the purple tint to her father's complexion—and noticing that Manningham's face was appearing calmer and calmer as he talked with his son, also an ominous sign—it occurred to Frederica that it behooved her to go slowly until she saw which way the land lay.

"I'm sorry, Father," Frederica said, her lovely head falling forward on her slender neck as she tried to appear the picture of contrition. "Heat of the moment, you know. My mind was on Anthony."

The earl harrumphed. "I find that," he told her, "remarkably hard to believe."

"But it was, Father!" Her head came up and her huge eyes gazed at him soulfully. "My mind has been totally filled with Anthony!" And how to get rid of him. She left the latter words unsaid, adding them only to salve her conscience as she crossed her fingers behind her back. "I have discovered I harbor feelings for him that I have tried for years to hide." She kept her fingers crossed as she hoped against hope that her father would not ask her what those feelings were.

Happily for Frederica, her father had never been as good at reading his children's expressions as was Anthony's.

"Well . . ." Forkham did not appear convinced but said no more. Manningham and Chilesworth approached, the former with a slight smile playing at his lips, the latter wearing a look that could only be described as direful.

The Earl of Manningham smiled for the benefit of the ladies, who were peeping at the four of them over their fans; and the gentlemen, who happened—just happened—to glance frequently in their direction and inch closer as inconspicuously as possible, to see what they might overhear. "Anthony informs me that he and Frederica have had a lover's spat," the earl said, his voice soft.

Frederica's father nodded. "Freddie says the same thing."

"Frederica." His daughter's correction was automatic, and she subsided as her father and Chilesworth glared at her.

"Ah, yes," Manningham said in his same soft voice, a hint of amusement in his eyes. "You have quite grown up on us, haven't you, Frederica?"

She swept him a graceful curtsy. "Years pass, my lord," she informed him, using her lashes to advantage, "and we change. All of us."

The earl agreed politely, but his son snorted. "Not always for the better," Chilesworth muttered.

Manningham gazed at him out of half-closed eyes. "Throwing stones, are you, Anthony? Being so pure yourself, of course . . ."

Chilesworth's color heightened as Frederica laughed. Her father glared at her.

"Try for a little decorum, Frederica," Forkham said.

"But of course, Papa." She curtsied to him. Manningham heard his son grind his teeth, and smiled.

"I believe, Anthony," Manningham said, "that you would like to dance with Frederica now."

"I would?" his heir repeated, surprised. Meeting his father's eyes, Chilesworth coughed and said, "Why, yes. Of course I would."

An equally surprised Frederica echoed "You would?" as he took her hand. Seeing the determined look on her father's face, she added, giving her betrothed her brightest smile, "Oh, Anthony! I am so sorry we quarreled! Let us never do so again!"

The viscount, about to sweep her out onto the dance floor, missed the step and had to begin again.

"Little minx," Frederica's father said, watching them join the waltzing couples who had decided the show, at least for the moment, appeared to be over and had returned to their dancing. Beside him, his friend laughed. "Ah, Giles," Manningham said, clapping a hand on his old friend's shoulder. "Whether or not we actually get them married, it promises to be a lively season, and no mistake!"

Anthony, watching his father and Frederica's over the top of her head, was relieved when he saw both gentlemen laugh. A small sigh escaped his lips, and Frederica, who did not have any view other than that of his cravat, looked up at him inquiringly. He grinned.

"Doing it a bit too brown, don't you think, Freddie?" he asked.

"Frederica," she said, correcting him again, then paused. "And I don't know what you mean!"

"'Oh, Anthony!'" he said, mimicking her, a high falsetto replacing his normal husky baritone. "Let us never quarrel again!"

Frederica giggled. "All right," she acknowledged. "But they seemed to accept it, didn't they?"

"Not for a minute." The viscount was cheerful as he disabused her of that notion. A small pucker appeared on Frederica's forehead.

"You think not?"

Chilesworth gave a good-natured smile as he gazed down at her. "Your father has known you for what—nineteen, twenty years now?—and you think he is taken in by that?"

"Twenty-two," Frederica informed him, a bit miffed that he did not remember such an important thing as her age. She knew him to be twenty-eight years and seven months, not that she cared or anything.

Chilesworth grinned. "So old?" he said mockingly. "No wonder your father is in a hurry to see you married!"

"It isn't my age—" Frederica began.

"No," the viscount agreed, "it's your reputation." Feeling her stiffen, he continued, his lips turning up in example. "Smile, my dear! Our fathers and most of Almack's are watching. And my father, I have come to know—often, oh, *often* to my sorrow—is alive to every trick."

Frederica nodded. "I have noticed that," she agreed, smiling brilliantly for the benefit of their audience. "And I have often wondered how you could be so different from him."

The viscount's smile was, for a moment, genuine. "I am alive to more tricks than you give me credit for, Freddie," he told her. "Never forget that."

"Frederica," she replied. He nodded. They danced for several moments in silence, smiling as if their lives depended on it.

"I do believe that if we must keep this up much longer, my face will crack," Chilesworth said at last, through gritted teeth. Frederica giggled.

"Courage, my hero!" she told him. "The dance can't last much longer."

"Then do you think we can separate?" His tone was so hopeful that she stepped on his foot. Again.

"Here now!" the viscount said, staring down at her. "What did you do that for?"

Frederica took her hand from his shoulder and laid it artistically against her forehead. "I'm sorry, Anthony," she said, the words subdued, "it must be my headache."

"Oh." Chilesworth's gaze was critical. "Not feeling quite the thing, are you? Thought when I first came in you weren't so much in looks tonight."

For a moment Frederica, who had spent three hours on her toilette earlier that evening just so he could see what he was missing, considered applying her toe to his shin rather than her heel to his instep. She counted to ten and did neither.

"No, you idiot," she said through lips that curled upward in determination. "I am only saying that I am developing a headache."

The viscount objected that that was no reason to get testy

with him, even going so far as to add that he hoped she didn't get like this every time she was a touch out of curl. Frederica forgot to smile as she said that it wasn't a *real* headache, it was a *pretend* headache—although if she had to spend much more time in his company, she could depend on it *becoming* real.

The viscount looked perplexed, and an exasperated Frederica explained that it was a headache guaranteed to get her taken home early.

"Oh." Chilesworth thought a moment. "I see.".

Frederica shook her head. "I doubt that, Anthony. I really do. But while you're seeing, see one more thing, will you? See that you stop by tomorrow to visit me. Perhaps it would be best if you took me for a drive. We need to talk."

"Can't," the viscount said. "You forget. I'm racing tomorrow."

Frederica, who had indeed forgotten, bit her lip. "Come after the race," she suggested.

"Can't. I'm engaged with friends."

"Friends more important than me, Anthony?" She said the words softly, favoring him with a look for which Mr. Mattington would have died. The viscount was not moved.

"Been promised to them for some time," he said.

"Anthony," Frederica said, just as the music slowed, "if you do not come to see me tomorrow, I will tell my father that it is all a hum, and he will tell your father—"

"I see." The viscount nodded, not looking at her as he appraised a lush beauty off to his right. "Developed a sudden fondness for Bath, have you?"

Frederica stared at him in surprise.

He smiled. "I'm willing to let you play your cards, Freddie," he told her gently, "but you don't hold all of them. Remember that."

The music stopped, and they stood for several moments gazing at each other. Their mothers, watching fondly, thought it was a soulful look they exchanged. Their fathers, watching with slightly more jaundiced eyes, thought it something else. At last the viscount said, "I'll come see you day after tomorrow. I'll take you driving then. I'll send round a note to tell you the time I'll be by. Plan on the morning. And don't be late—I won't keep my horses standing!"

"Well!" Frederica said, but was stopped by the viscount's caution to smile. She did, once again conscious of her father's and the Earl of Manningham's close scrutiny. Anthony, his own lips turned up in a determined grimace the world might interpret as a smile if it so chose, led her back to her mother, who was seated by the Countess of Manningham. Both ladies beamed up at them.

"Frederica, my darling! You are in such looks tonight!" Lady Manningham cried, rising to give her future daughter-in-law a hug. Frederica flashed a triumphant glance in the viscount's direction as that young man's mother continued. "It must be the happiness showing through! I know, for I am so happy too!"

"Are you, my lady?" was all Frederica could think to say. Happiness, indeed!

Chilesworth grinned. "Frederica has developed a head-ache, Mama," he said, smiling down at the older ladies in that heart-stopping way Frederica felt had a most ill-judged effect on females of all ages. Instantly they were solicitous.

"It must be the excitement of the day," Frederica's mother said, putting an arm around her daughter's shoulders.

"Yes, Mama." Frederica tried her best to achieve suitably faint tones. "It must be."

"Too bad," Lady Manningham said, fluttering. "Too, too bad . . . on this, the night of your betrothal."

Frederica sighed, eyes lowered. "Yes," she said. "My betrothal. Too, too bad." Neither of the older ladies understood why Anthony chuckled.

"We must take you home at once," Frederica's mother declared. Her daughter raised appealing eyes to her.

"Oh, Mama, would you? I do so hate to leave early, but . . ." She let the words trail off so the ladies could interpret her disappointment as they chose.

"There will be other dances, Frederica." Chilesworth's words and tone were gallant, causing both his mother and Frederica's to smile approvingly. "I shall look forward to them."

"I'm sure you will," she said, her eyes suggesting that he would look forward to dancing them with someone else, and that she would enjoy the same. The viscount grinned.

"Until we meet again." He bowed over Frederica's hand with a rare grace that Mr. Mattington, watching from afar, could only envy with all his heart, then placed a warm kiss on her wrist.

Frederica's mother sighed. "How romantic!" the countess said, favoring Anthony with yet another smile.

"Yes." Frederica's frown, the ladies decided, was due to her headache. "How very, very romantic!"

Chapter
Ten

THE NEXT DAY—the day of Anthony's race—found Frederica hard put to settle down with any of her normal activities. With her future hanging in the balance, such things as embroidery or reading or even going out to purchase a new hat seemed more trivial than she would ever, seventy-two hours earlier, have thought possible.

Plus the day was gray as her mood, which was not improved by the continual stream of visitors who filed through the Earl and Countess of Forkham's doors, each intent on ferreting out what they could of this most interesting piece of news concerning the Lady Frederica Farthingham's engagement to the Viscount Chilesworth. Frederica, who felt like kicking and screaming each time either betrothals or viscounts were mentioned, had to sit with a polite smile fixed on her lips while she parried inquisitive questions as best she could, and while her mother smiled proudly and told everyone who would listen—and that was everyone who came—that it was a love match.

Frederica, sipping tea the first time she heard those words come out of her mother's mouth, choked and dropped her cup, which landed on the floor with a loud clatter. Instantly a footman appeared to clean up the mess. Noting the dark tea stains spattering her hem, Frederica hastily excused herself to go change her dress.

"Isn't that always the way it is?" she heard her mother say fondly to old Mrs. Batterington, who was one of the ton's most inveterate gossips and who had appeared on their doorstep as early as could possibly be considered polite. "I remember when I was first engaged to dear Giles—it's a wonder my mother had a cup left in the house, I was so clumsy! One's mind goes wandering, you know."

Frederica, who had never heard such whiskers coming from her mother's mouth before—and so calmly too—thought rather that it was the truth that had gone wandering, and taxed her mother with that when they next were alone. The countess's face was calm as she regarded her daughter.

"Why, Frederica," Lady Forkham said, opening her eyes wide, a trick that always served her well and one which Frederica had learned early to imitate—usually with the same results. "I don't know what you mean."

Frederica frowned at her.

"Oh, no, Mama," Frederica said. "You know very well that that wide-eyed look doesn't work with me." Her mother smiled. "And you know very well what I mean, so don't be pretending that you don't!"

The countess raised a questioning eyebrow, and Frederica's frown grew.

"Telling Mrs. Batterington, who will have it all over town in less than a day, that our engagement is a love match! And you don't even bat an eye!"

With gentle fingers, the countess smoothed the lace that trimmed the sleeves of her dark blue morning dress and gave her daughter a fond smile. "But, Frederica," Lady Forkham objected. "I told Mrs. Batterington nothing but the truth. It *is* a love match! *I* love this match, and your *father* loves this match, and *Anthony's parents* love this match." She slanted her daughter a considering glance and smoothed the lace again. "And just last night you and Chilesworth told your fathers you'd been mistaken in your feelings for each other and now find—" She broke off when she heard the knocker fall on the front door.

Frederica rolled her eyes and bit her lip. "I suppose that is someone else come to wish me happy—and to pry!"

"I would imagine it is," her mother agreed in that calm voice that Frederica found most exasperating. "And if you don't wish them to go away with more to talk about than you bargained for, my dear, you will smile and try not to spill your tea each time I answer an impertinence with an . . . ah . . . let us say, exaggeration."

The countess almost blushed, but Frederica was prevented from pouncing on this near admission that her mother knew she was telling less than the truth by the entrance of Higgins, come to announce Lady Sarah Ogglesby and her daughter, Susan. Since Lady Ogglesby had tried without success the better part of the previous year to bring Susan to Chilesworth's notice, it was not to be expected that she or her daughter actually came with the idea of wishing the betrothed couple well. Frederica, trying her best to give nothing away under Lady Ogglesby's sharp eyes, accepted without a blink her mother's placid tale of a love match and even managed a becoming blush—although George, had he been present, would have known at once it was anger, rather than embarrassment, staining his sister's cheeks.

Susan asked just how the viscount had proposed.

"Oh, Susan," Frederica said, looking away in what she hoped might be mistaken for maidenly embarrassment, "I cannot tell you that!"

"Why not?" her inquisitor demanded.

"Because!" Frederica replied, and there was a warning light in her eye that her mother saw. The countess closed her eyes tight, waiting for an explosion; when it did not come, she opened her eyes again to find Frederica regarding her thoughtfully.

"Because," Frederica said, still watching her mother, "it is between Anthony and me!"

Susan sniffed. "Well, I've heard for several years that there was something between you and Chilesworth, Frederica!" the young woman said, her eyes narrowed and her color heightened. "But I never heard it was a love match!"

"But how would you?" Frederica's return was swift, and she fairly purred the words. At her tone the countess closed her eyes again and waited. "It's not as if you are among dear Anthony's intimates, now is it?"

"Well!" Lady Ogglesby gasped. Susan sat rigid, two spots of color burning high on her cheeks. Frederica, her own face betraying a slight flush, waited with relish for what either of the Ogglesby ladies might say next, but the conversation was turned by Frederica's mother, who, as if the preceding exchange had never occurred, smiled brightly at everyone present and asked if they would like more tea.

It was after the Ogglesby ladies left that a thoughtful Lady Forkham said she now understood her daughter still had the headache that had plagued her the previous night, and that she—the countess—would quite understand if Frederica did not care to be at home to any more of the visitors they would be receiving that day.

Frederica looked at her in surprise. "But, Mama," she began, "I do not have the headache—"

"Yes, Frederica." Her mother's voice was firm. "You do. And not only do you have it, but I fear it is contagious. I can tell that if I spend much more time in your presence today, I will have it too!"

"Oh." Frederica understood and sought to justify herself. "Well, she started it—"

Lady Forkham, while agreeing that the provocation had been great and that she had not really minded the novelty of seeing the Ogglesby ladies for once bereft of words, still let it be known that too much more such novelty in one day would be more than she cared to take.

"Oh." Frederica rose. "Well, perhaps I shall go riding."

"Not with a headache," her mother told her.

"But—"

"My dear, I cannot tell our guests that you are indisposed with a headache when they might then meet you in Hyde Park looking remarkably well!"

Frederica saw the logic in that and bit her lip. "It is all Anthony's fault!" she said. "If he weren't out racing that stupid race, we could get this settled—" She stopped suddenly, aware of what she'd said, and aware, too, that her mother was regarding her with keen interest.

"Get what settled, Frederica?" the countess asked as the knocker was heard again on the mansion's front door.

Frederica, looking toward the sound, put a hand to her forehead and rubbed her temple. "Do you know, Mama," she said, "I do believe you are right. I *do* have the headache, and if you will excuse me . . ." She crossed to the door leading into her father's study as she and Lady Forkham heard Higgins leading their newest guests down the hall.

"Frederica!" the countess said, but it was too late; already her daughter had slipped through the door and was gone. As Higgins opened the hall morning-room door Lady Forkham schooled her face to a look of polite delight at the sight of her newest guests and requested that the butler bring them a new pot of tea.

It didn't take long before the day seemed interminable to Frederica, who moved from her bedchamber to the library and even to the kitchen in search of—well, she didn't really know *what* she was in search of. There was a restlessness in her that was most uncomfortable, and she wished for the thousandth time that Anthony had canceled that stupid race and come to her when she had asked him to. She also wished that the small, whispering voice in her head, which said that Anthony canceling the race would not have been reasonable, would develop laryngitis and go away.

She was barred from the diversion of chatting with her mother in the morning room by the steady stream of visitors who appeared there. Once, after a trip to the kitchen in search of company—a trip that so flustered the chef's assistant that he dropped a bowl and was soundly berated for it by the chef, for which Frederica was sorry—she considered a miraculous recovery from her headache. Then she could rejoin her mother and their guests.

Her consideration of a recovery lasted only a few moments. Down the hall, she heard Higgins announce the Misses Guildthorpe, and she almost felt a real headache coming on. The Misses Guildthorpe were known both for their gossiping and for the incessant titterings and tongue cluckings that accompanied even the simplest of their sentences. With a sigh Frederica took herself off to the library, and was searching for a book when her father entered the room.

"Ah, Frederica!" the earl said, beaming at her. "I am glad to see you up and about! Your mother tells me you have a headache!"

"Yes, Father, I do, and I am likely to have it as long as . . . as . . ." Behind her father she saw, too late, the Earl of Manningham and ended in what sounded lame even to her own ears. "As long as it remains so gray, I suppose."

Frederica's father was quick to accept that, but sudden comprehension appeared in Manningham's eyes, and he disconcerted her by coming forward to take her hand and bow over it. He placed a gentle kiss upon her wrist before straightening to say, his voice soft, "I wish you a speedy recovery, Frederica."

"Oh!"

The surprised Frederica put the hand to her cheek as her

father said in his good-natured way, "Oh, nothing to worry about! Freddie is never sick! She'll be right as a trivet in no time."

"I hope so," Manningham murmured. For a moment Frederica perceived an elusive likeness between the earl and his son and was further disconcerted. Feeling her cheeks grow pink, she said that she would not disturb them, she was not good company today, and besides, she was sure they wished to be alone.

Picking a book at random from a shelf, she hurried from the room and up the back stairs to her bedchamber. If it wasn't bad enough that Anthony *didn't* come today, it was even worse that his father *did*, she thought crossly. Her mood was not improved when she flung herself into her chair and with determination opened the book she'd brought with her, only to find it an old book of sermons on the proper place of women in the home and in society. Since it focused a great deal on the need for humility and patience and a bowing to the will of others, it was not surprising that Frederica did not read for long.

By evening Frederica's enforced inactivity and continuing anxiety had made her increasingly edgy. Pleading a throbbing headache that was becoming more truth than fiction, Frederica ate supper with her parents but declined to accompany them to a musicale at Lord and Lady Symington's. After looking thoughtfully at her daughter for several moments Lady Forkham acquiesced to Frederica's wishes.

"I'll just go to bed early," Frederica told them as the three stood in the mansion hallway. She watched her father wrap the countess's cloak about her and give his wife's shoulder a friendly squeeze as he did so. For some reason the way her mother smiled up at the earl made a lump grow in Frederica's throat, although she'd seen them exchange that look of warm intimacy countless times before. Lady Forkham, chancing to see Frederica's face, included her daughter in the lovely smile.

"Yes, do, dear," her mother urged. "For you wouldn't want your headache to linger into tomorrow."

There was gentle meaning behind the words, and Frederica nodded.

"After all," her mother continued, "Anthony is to come tomorrow, isn't he?"

Her father, hearing, turned and said, a huge grin upon his face, "Oh, yes! Meant to tell you, my dear! Anthony won his race today. Manningham told me when he was here. Of course, we knew he'd win, didn't we? Ran it bang up to the mark, and neither he nor his team a bit the worse for wear of it."

"You mean"—Frederica's look was incredulous as she gazed at her father—"Anthony's race was run by the time his father was here this afternoon?"

The warning pinch his wife delivered to his arm meant nothing to Forkham, so he ignored it. "Of course!" he said, gazing at his daughter in surprise. "Well it stands to reason Manningham wouldn't have come until after he'd seen the finish, now doesn't it?"

"B-but I thought," Frederica said, stuttering, "that Chilesworth was to be late. Engaged with friends, for supper, he said. I thought . . ."

The earl, not understanding the emotion moving his daughter, strove to reassure her. "Now, Freddie," he told her, "it's like I said. The race is run, and neither he nor his team are one whit the worse for wear!"

Frederica, her eyes snapping as her father ushered her mother out the door, was pleased for Anthony's horses. As for the viscount, however . . .

The viscount's well-being was a very different matter!

Chapter
Eleven

VISCOUNT CHILESWORTH ARRIVED early the next day to take his betrothed driving, or he might have missed her. Frederica had decided, after much tossing and turning the night before, that if his lordship could not squeeze her into his schedule except when it was quite convenient for him, he would find that she, too, had other things to do than sit and await him. So it was that he was just pulling up in front of the mansion when Frederica, accompanied by her maid, stepped out the door, intent on some shopping.

"Oh, there you are," Chilesworth said as his groom ran to the heads of the horses to hold them. "Most prompt. But when I said you weren't to keep me waiting, Frederica, I didn't mean you had to meet me on the sidewalk!"

The latter was said with great humor but drew a chilly reception from the lady. Jumping lightly down from the phaeton, Anthony took one critical look at Frederica's face and said, with more feeling than tact, "Oh. Out of curl again, are you?"

Frederica's tone was tart as she informed him it was no such thing. Then she added, nose in the air, "But I find I cannot accompany you now, Anthony. I have some shopping to do that cannot wait. You will have to come back."

"Come back?" Chilesworth echoed, looking from her to her maid to his horses to the groom standing at their heads. His attention returned to Frederica. "When you were so insistent that I come to you as soon as possible? Don't be ridiculous!"

Frederica let it be know that it was not *she* who was ridiculous, adding, for good measure, that that was not a gentlemanly thing to say. Viscount Chilesworth, a warning light in his eye, said that he was not feeling quite as gentlemanly as she might like.

"Well, I do not doubt it!" Frederica cried, glaring up at him. "Not that you ever are! For no *gentleman* requested by a lady to call upon her at his earliest convenience would wait more than a day to do so when he had several hours between appointments but simply chose to go off with his friends as if he were twelve again and no doubt participate in stupid and irresponsible and childish things."

For a moment Chilesworth's brow furrowed in puzzlement; then it cleared, and amusement showed in his face as he said, taking her arm, "Ah. I see. Not used to being kept waiting are you, Freddie?"

"*Frederica!*" she corrected, pulling away from him and stuffing the free hand he would have taken into her muff. "And I am *never* kept waiting—at least not by a *gentleman!*"

The emphasis on the last word was not lost on him and regrettably, the viscount laughed. Frederica, wanting to hit him, settled on wishing him a cold "Good day." She began to walk by him, her wide-eyed maid on her heels. Both women were startled a moment later when the viscount swept Frederica up into his arms and started with her toward the phaeton.

"Put me down!" Frederica said, hitting him with her muff.

Chilesworth grinned at her. "But no, Freddie," he said, "that would be too bad of me. For I have come to take you

driving—on the day I promised, and even earlier than I said
I'd arrive—and it would be most *ungentlemanly* of me to
fail to keep our appointment."

"My lord . . ." Frederica's maid began as the front door
of the mansion opened. The maid, Frederica, and the
viscount paused and looked toward the house as George
stepped out. Frederica's brother stopped a moment at
sight of the strange tableau before him; then, straightening
his hat carefully on his head, he shut the door behind
him and came down the walk, whistling and twirling his
cane.

"Good morning, Frederica," George said, as if he saw
his sister in his best friend's arms every morning of the year.
He tipped his hat. "Good morning, Anthony."

Viscount Chilesworth grinned. "Good morning, George.
You are looking remarkably well after such a late night."

"Not as well as you" came his friend's gallant reply.
Frederica stared at her brother.

"George!" she protested.

Handsomely he said that she looked the best of them all.

"*George!!!*" Frederica repeated. He turned an inquiring
eye her way.

"Chilesworth is holding me, George!"

Her brother looked them over carefully. "Yes," he said.
"Yes, he is."

Frederica took a deep breath. "Against my will,
George."

"Oh." Her brother gave that pronouncement deep
thought. "Is he now?"

Frederica assured him that he was.

"Oh." George said it again and gave a resigned sigh.

"I don't suppose you'd care to put her down?" George
questioned, turning his inquiring gaze toward his friend.

Chilesworth said he would not.

"Didn't think so." George gave his head a sad shake.
"Well, I suppose there is only one thing for it, then."

Turning, George handed his hat to the openmouthed maid, who stood watching this unusual scene. Turning back toward his sister and his friend, he shouted, "En garde!" and, raising his cane like a sword, advanced upon the viscount.

"George!" shrieked Frederica as a laughing Chilesworth kept her firmly clamped to his chest, bobbing and weaving to avoid his friend's thrusts. "George, stop that!"

Obediently her brother did, and Frederica frowned from one to the other of the men. "I thought better of you, George!" She sniffed, trying to right her hat, which had gone sadly askew in the excitement. Her brother managed a suitable crestfallen expression and Chilesworth chuckled. Again Frederica hit him with her muff. "Put me down, you big gudgeon!" she said. The viscount took another step toward the phaeton.

"Did you not think better of me, too, my dear?" he asked. A frosty Frederica informed him that whenever possible she did not think of him at all. Behind her, George laughed as Anthony tossed her up onto the phaeton seat and nimbly climbed up after her.

"George!" Frederica appealed, looking back at her brother. "George, do something!"

George did. He asked where Anthony was taking his sister, and seemed more reassured than Frederica when the viscount replied, "On a drive to Richmond—or to wring her pretty little neck. I shall decide soon which it is to be."

Then, telling his groom he need not accompany them, Chilesworth gave the team the office to start and they were off, Frederica's maid calling, "But, my lord . . . but, my lord . . ." behind them.

Frederica, sitting stiff and erect, the color in her cheeks high, said, "There is no reason to go to Richmond, Anthony. A turn around Hyde Park will be quite enough."

"Oh, I don't think so," said the maddening figure beside

her. "We could never quarrel really well together in a turn around Hyde Park, now could we?"

Frederica favored him with her best glare as she said in icily civil tones that if he was of a mind to be quarrelsome, he could set her down right there.

"Oh, not me, Freddie," he said. "You. I am thinking of you, my dear. You never could quarrel really well with me in the park when you were forever having to stop to greet various acquaintances."

"My name," the lady said, her tone dangerous, "is Frederica. And I am *not* of a quarrelsome nature."

The viscount laughed.

"Besides," Frederica said, "you dismissed your groom. We have no chaperon with us."

The viscount said that he hadn't thought they could quarrel really well in front of a chaperon, either. He added, with a sidelong glance, that as an affianced couple they did not need a chaperon on such a fine day. Frederica, adjusting her hat, fixed a jaundiced eye upon the sky and said it looked as if it might rain.

"Then I suppose we will get wet!" her betrothed responded. His voice carried a blithe cheerfulness she was fast coming to detest.

"And catch our death of cold and die of an inflammation of the lungs!" Frederica snapped. "I suppose you would like that, Anthony!"

"Well, at least it would solve this engagement problem, wouldn't it?" the viscount replied in the same cheerful tone. He chuckled when Frederica turned a cold shoulder his way and gazed pointedly out at the passing scene. After several moments of bowling along in silence the viscount reached into his pocket and pulled out a small packet of paper. He tapped her on the shoulder and, when he had her attention, handed it to her.

"Why, what is this?" Frederica was surprised as she stared down at the pound notes.

"Your winnings," he said.

"But . . ." She looked from the money to him. "How did you . . . ?"

"I collected your winnings for you, Frederica," he said. "After the race."

"Oh. Well." She was more surprised. "That was very nice—" She stopped and thought. "But how did you know who my wager was with?" she asked.

He ignored the question as he frowned at her. "Never bet with the baron again, Frederica," he said. "I won't have it."

She stared at him for several moments as surprise turned to anger. "*You* won't have it? And what do *you* have to say about it, I'd like to know? And why who I bet with is any of your business—"

"I have a great deal to say about it," Chilesworth said, interrupting. "As your future husband I have a great deal to say about everything. Do not bet with the baron, Frederica. He is not the type of man I would have you associate with."

He is not the type of man I would have you associate with . . .

Frederica had heard those words before, uttered by the viscount in nearly the same tone, and she froze. All at once she was eighteen again, giddy with the success of her first season. She had attracted the attention of Lord Nettleton, known for his rakish ways—and known, too, to detest silly schoolgirls. Since he had joined her court, Frederica, just out, was more than a little flattered and quite pleased to consider herself a woman of vast sophistication. She had turned a deaf ear to her mother's gentle warnings and George's more sarcastic ones and had allowed Nettleton to lead her a little aside one day at the Manningham alfresco party—to see the fish pond, Nettleton had said. It had been a lovely, sky-blue day, and she was wearing her newest gown, her favorite, cerulean blue. Lord Nettleton had said she put the sky to shame. . . .

Frederica sighed. Lord Nettleton had tried to kiss her, once out of sight of the party. He had grown quite insistent when she refused, and they had been struggling when Anthony came around the hedge.

Without ado, Chilesworth had dumped Lord Nettleton into the fish pond, recommending that the other man take a damper. Frederica, relieved, had turned to Anthony to thank him, but before she could tell the viscount of her gratitude, Chilesworth, who had found himself disproportionately angry at the sight of Frederica struggling in Nettleton's arms, had marched her away, lecturing in a scalding tone on her morals, sense, and what he called (most unfairly, she thought) her fast and flirtatious ways. In minutes Frederica's gratitude turned to indignation and then to burning anger.

By the time the viscount paused for breath, Frederica had forgotten all about saying thank you and, her nerves as jangling as his, she wanted only to rip up at him as he was ripping at her. She proceeded to do so, recalling every transgression of the viscount's from the age of nine (and she found, when she dwelt on it, that they were many). She ended her rebuttal with the statement that Viscount Chilesworth was not in the position to tell *anyone*—especially a well-bred young lady like herself—how to behave, and that he might take himself off and never speak to her again.

She had hoped then that he would apologize so that she could, and that he might hand her his handkerchief, for Frederica felt an overwhelming desire to cry. But Chilesworth, his young face murderous, had bowed in the most icily civil manner possible and stalked off.

Lord Nettleton had taken a prolonged tour of the continent shortly thereafter, to regain his dignity—something hard to do after a ducking in a fish pond, although only Frederica and Anthony knew about it. When Nettleton and

Frederica met in company these days, they passed with no more than a common bow. Nettleton was not, she had found, the type of man she cared to associate with, anyway.

Still, Anthony should not have tried to come so heavy-handed over her, and this ridiculous belief he had that he could dictate who she might associate with—it was not to be borne! So she glared up at him now and said huffily, "Well! Of all the . . . And we are *not* to be married, Anthony, so who I do or do not associate with—although why you dislike the baron so, when I find him *très amusant*—"

"Amusing?" Chilesworth repeated. "*Amusing?* For goodness sake, Freddie—"

Frederica, realizing that this line of conversation was getting them nowhere closer to a solution to their problem, held up a hand and said, in the role of peacemaker, "I'll tell you what, Anthony. As long as we are engaged, I will not wager with the baron."

"Or have anything to do with him," Chilesworth said.

Frederica bit her lip. "I will not wager with him," she repeated. Then she added, as the viscount looked mulish, "After all, it is not as if he comes very much in my way."

A frowning Anthony drove in silence for several moments before saying abruptly, "What do you mean, 'as long as we're engaged'? If you have a plan to get us out of this, Freddie, I wish you'd tell me. You keep hinting at one but—"

"Frederica!" she snapped. "And yes, I have a plan. Which I would have told you yesterday, had you come to call."

Her brow darkened at thought of his perfidy, and he rolled his eyes. "I believe we have been over all that," he said. "I dance to no woman's piping, and certainly not to yours."

"Well!" Frederica said. "I shall be heartily sorry for the poor soul who does one day enter into matrimony with you!"

The viscount grinned. "You never *used* to be one of those females forever feeling sorry for herself, Freddie."

"Frederica!" she cried. "And I am not speaking about myself."

The viscount's gaze was distinctly skeptical. He had no intention of moving to Brazil. "Spill it, my dear," he advised, "and we'll see."

Chapter
Twelve

IT WAS, FREDERICA told him, quite simple; since their fathers were so determined that they continue with this engagement or suffer their respective banishments, they would do so. For a time. As a ruse.

"A ruse?" Chilesworth's skepticism increased.

Frederica nodded. They would pretend to be engaged, she said, in order to give them both time to look around for someone else to marry.

"But I don't want to marry!" the viscount objected.

Frederica told him she did not wish to do so, either; but if her father was so set on pushing her into wedlock, she at least wanted to choose the person with whom she entered the married state.

"Sounds like a hum to me," Anthony said.

Frederica frowned at him. "Do you have a better idea?"

He thought for a moment, found he did not, but raised further objections. "The thing is," he said, "what if you find someone to marry and I don't?"

Frederica said that either way it would work; he might find someone or she might find someone or they both might find someone; in any of those situations their en-

gagement to each other would be at an end. The viscount
hooted.

"And I suppose you think your father is going to say
'Thank you very much' when you waltz into his study one
day with the news that you've found yourself a husband—
and it's not the man you're betrothed to?" He thought a
moment, then whistled low. "I know what *my* father would
say, were I to bring him such tidings, and I don't want to
hear it!"

Frederica's forehead puckered; it was apparent she hadn't
considered that angle of her plan.

"And besides," Anthony continued, watching her, "it's
not as if I want the whole town talking and laughing
behind my back and saying you threw me over for another
man!"

Frederica's voice was cold as she said she didn't understand why he cared for that, as long as it got him what he
wanted, which was out of the betrothal. Anthony wasn't
sure why he cared for that, either, but he did.

"Besides," Frederica said, "your father will no doubt feel
so sorry for you, if I find someone else and you don't, that
he won't press you to marry for—oh, ages!"

Anthony made it clear he did not want his father feeling
sorry for him, either.

"And another thing. . . ." Frederica was thinking aloud
and ignoring his contrary interruptions. "If it is you who
finds a suitable partner and not me, then *my* father will feel
sorry for *me* and likely will not try to pressure me into
another engagement."

It was apparent Frederica did not find the idea of her
father feeling sorry for her as repugnant as did her betrothed. "Oh, Anthony!" Without thinking she clasped his
arm. "Would you?"

"Would I what?" he asked, looking down at her small
hands. She beamed up at him. "Would you please find
someone to fall madly in love with and carry her off to

Gretna Green and leave me behind as your brokenhearted fiancée?"

She appeared so delighted with the thought that he gave his arm an irritable shake. That startled his horses, and they broke into a gallop. Instantly they were checked as the viscount said crossly that no, no he would not.

"I ain't a jilt," he said flatly.

"But I would not mind!" Her face was earnest as Frederica assured him that, far from being truly broken-hearted, she would consider him a hero and be eternally grateful.

"Well, you needn't be," Chilesworth assured her, "because I ain't a jilt and I ain't soft in the head and I ain't carrying anybody off to Gretna Green!" He snorted. "A fine thing that would be!"

Frederica, stung, said that it *would* be a fine thing—it would be a very fine thing indeed. "And you *are* soft in the head!" she said, correcting him, "and—a—a pudding heart too! Just for the lack of a little resolution you wish to *ruin* my life—"

"Ruin your life!" the viscount repeated. "Ruin *your* life? Oh, you're a fine one to talk, my girl! As if it would brighten every one of my remaining days to be tied to *you* through eternity! I tell you, Freddie, Brazil sounds better every day!"

Her gaze was speculative and for once she ignored the shortening of her name. After a moment she sighed in disappointment and her face fell. "I didn't think you meant it."

"Meant what?" Chilesworth asked, looking down at her.

"That you were ready to go to Brazil."

"Of course I ain't going to Brazil."

Frederica sighed again. "Well, then," she asked, "what do you propose we do?"

Chilesworth frowned forward for several moments, his

attention riveted on his horses' ears. "Well," he said at last, "I suppose we could get married."

"*What?*"

He continued to stare straight ahead. "It might do, Freddie," he said. "You might like being a married lady. I wouldn't be tight-pursed or anything. And as long as you didn't interfere with my life—"

"Or you with mine."

He frowned at her. "What do you mean by that?"

"What did *you* mean?" she countered.

He reddened. "That has nothing to do—"

"It has *everything* to do!" Frederica told him. "Because if you think that you can go on carousing and carrying on with . . . with opera dancers and ladybirds—"

A grinning viscount asked just what she knew about opera dancers and ladybirds.

"Then so can I!"

His grin grew. "You want to carouse with opera dancers, Freddie?" he asked.

"Frederica!" she almost screamed. "And you know perfectly well what I meant!"

Chilesworth's grin disappeared and he sat up very straight. "I certainly do, and no wife of mine is going to behave in such a way."

"Well, I'm not going to be your wife," Frederica said. "And that's a very good thing!"

"It certainly is!"

They glared at each other for several moments more, and Chilesworth at last gave a grudging sigh. "Oh, all right," he told her. "I don't think it will work, mind you, but once more, tell me your plan."

Frederica did. She repeated it again and again, and although Chilesworth objected, and remained clearly skeptical, she had the satisfaction of knowing, when he returned her to her home that afternoon, that if she had not fully convinced him that it was the best way out of their predicament, she had at least won his grudging agreement that it might be worth a try.

"Now remember," she cautioned him as he pulled his team to a halt before the Earl of Forkham's London home, "no one must suspect. We must appear to get along famously."

The viscount objected that only a dolt or a cad would try to court someone known to be engaged and who seemed to get along famously with his or her betrothed. Frederica fluttered her eyelashes at him.

"Sometimes, Anthony," she told him, "a person's feelings can be so strong that he is willing to go to great lengths to win her love."

"Hmmph!" said the viscount.

Frederica's mouth tightened. "All right," she said. "We must get along well enough that our parents will think we have accepted this betrothal nonsense, but not so well that no one else might think he has a chance."

"Or she?" Chilesworth asked.

"Or she," Frederica agreed.

The viscount shook his head pessimistically. "It won't work," he told her.

Frederica, in the process of handing herself down from his phaeton, since he could not help her because his groom had been dismissed and the viscount had to hold his own horses, frowned up at him and said, "It will."

"You haven't found anyone who took your fancy in the past three years," he told her. "What makes you think you're going to do so now?"

"I will put my mind to it."

The viscount smiled, a curious little smile that touched a secret place in his eyes. "Do you think you can do everything you put your mind to?"

By now she was standing on firm ground. Surprised by the question, she turned her wide violet gaze upon him. "Well . . ." She chewed her lip for a moment, then her shoulders went back in the position of a fighter and her face grew determined. "At least if I don't, it won't be because I didn't try!"

Chilesworth nodded and gave his horses the direction to start. Behind him, he heard Frederica call, "And you must try, too, Anthony! Don't forget!" He made no response as he bowled down the avenue toward his own home.

Chapter Thirteen

FOR THE NEXT month Anthony and Frederica kept to their agreed-upon plan. Their faces were wreathed in radiant smiles whenever they found themselves together in company, which was often. Both were popular among the ton and were invited to the same parties, balls, and musicales. Also, both knew that if they did not spend a certain amount of time with each other, their esteemed parents, not yet appearing totally convinced of their children's apparent about-face, would have their suspicions aroused.

In private, however, the viscount's and Frederica's foreheads more often were decorated with frowns, and they seemed to quarrel royally over anything and everything, ranging from the feather in Frederica's hat to Chilesworth's tendency to assume a superior air because he was superior in height to his betrothed.

Now, as they drove around Hyde Park, smiling and nodding at their acquaintances, they kept up a low-pitched argument no one else could hear, the viscount having dismissed his groom so that he might chastise his betrothed without restraint.

"And that's another thing," Chilesworth said, revolted as Frederica gave her best smile and wave of the hand as the two bowled past Mr. Mattington, soberly riding the path on a hired hack. The young man's face lit up, and Anthony's frown deepened. "Why must you continue to encourage that young jackanapes? It's beyond me! Coming it a bit too brown, Frederica, if you think anyone will believe you might prefer that—that puppy to me!"

The face Frederica turned toward Chilesworth did not carry the same smile she'd given Mr. Mattington.

"Do you think so, Anthony?" she asked, as if considering her words. "Would it be so difficult for the ton to believe that a lady might prefer a gentleman who is always kind and considerate of her, who has her comforts in mind and procures her a glass of champagne when she is thirsty and fetches her shawl when she is chilly and who never argues with her—"

She got no further, for the viscount, whose mouth was opening and closing, could contain himself no longer. "Good lord," he said, "he really *is* a puppy!"

Frederica glared at him. "Mr. Mattington," she said, "is a kindhearted young man—not that he is so very young, because we are of the same age! And . . ." She turned her head away to smile at Lady Jersey, who smiled back, her narrow gaze suggesting that she could read the emotions of Viscount Chilesworth and his betrothed better than many of those taking the air in the park. "I enjoy his company."

That, at least, was true. Frederica did enjoy Mr. Mattington's company. His was an uncomplicated presence, and after any time spent in Chilesworth's vicinity she was warmed by the genuine admiration that lit Mr. Mattington's face each time he saw her. Mr. Mattington never had an uncomplimentary word to say about the color of her dress, as the viscount had last Thursday, seeming to think that being betrothed gave him the right to dispute her fashion sense. That Chilesworth's opinion had been the same as that voiced earlier by her mother and her dresser still rankled with Frederica.

Mr. Mattington never told her to take a damper, or that she was trying him too far, or that she was foolish to risk her gold bracelet in a game of silver loo.

She flushed as she remembered how Anthony, coming into the room just as she'd stripped the bracelet from her wrist and laid it on the table, sauntered over to stand behind her chair. After watching critically for a moment he had picked the bracelet up and said, his tone smooth, "Let me stake you, my darling. I am sure this bracelet could not grace anyone's lovely arm as well as it does yours."

The smile he had turned on the other ladies at the table robbed his words of any sting, but Frederica still seethed. It did not help that she had wished the moment she staked the bracelet that she had not, had sought a face-saving way out of the situation and had found none. She should have been grateful to Anthony for saving face for her, but curiously she was not. And she had won; she convinced herself she *knew* she would win, else she would not have staked the bracelet. She had told Anthony that, but he had given her one of those enigmatic looks that always made her long to hit the person turning it upon her, and had said one could never depend on winning at the tables, and one should never play unless one had pocket money to lose. Frederica had already lost her pocket money that night, but she had not wanted to tell him that, feeling it might further prove his point, and so . . .

She was recalled from her thoughts by Chilesworth's hand on her arm. Looking down, she was distracted by the warmth that seemed to transfer from his gloved fingers to her wrist. She gazed up, startled, to find herself the subject of his close regard.

"You haven't heard a word I've said these past five minutes, have you?" he asked.

Frederica removed her hand from under his. "You said you did not wish me to be seen in Mr. Mattington's company," she told him, her head held high. "I say, *ha!*"

The viscount nodded. "You *haven't* been paying attention," he informed her. "What I said is that no one could believe you prefer Mattington to me, but if you wish to encourage the poor fellow, I won't forbid it."

"Forbid?" Frederica gasped the word.

Chilesworth ignored her. "Although, if you have a kindness for him, you might have a thought for his feelings. Encouraging him as you have, he might start to believe you care for him more than you do."

Frederica almost flushed. That thought had occurred to her, too, and she was trying her best to make it clear to Mr. Mattington that while she enjoyed his company, she sought nothing more from him than friendship. Although in the face of her censorious betrothed, Mr. Mattington's undying devotion wouldn't hurt, either . . . just to soothe her feelings.

Frederica sighed, knowing she needed to think about that more. All thoughts of Mr. Mattington were driven from her head by the viscount's next statement, however.

"The person I *do* forbid you to encourage is Baron Barnsley," Chilesworth said, his voice and face as calm as if he'd just told Frederica he hoped she was enjoying the beautiful day.

The lady's jaw tightened. "In the first place," she said, nodding at Lord and Lady Byrington as their carriage passed the viscount's phaeton, "I do not *encourage* Baron Barnsley."

"Oho!" the viscount hooted. "And who was it who danced twice with him last night at the Symington ball?"

"Any number of ladies, I would imagine!" Frederica snapped. "I was not watching!"

"Well, I was," the viscount informed her, "and he only danced twice with one woman. In fact, you're the only woman he danced with all night."

"What?" The surprise in Frederica's face was real, and Chilesworth's frown relaxed. He paused a moment to lift his hat to Lady Stelton, then returned his gaze to Frederica. She was experiencing the flattery of finding she had been the only one to receive the baron's charming attentions—for he had been at his best, charming and witty and ready to attend to her every comfort, putting himself out to please—and the added surprise of finding that Anthony had noticed.

"I know there are times, Freddie, that you don't realize what you are doing—" he began. It was an unfortunate choice of words, for Frederica had heard them before from her father and brother and had always resented the words coming out of their mouths. She certainly was not going to listen to them from Viscount Chilesworth!

"You are wrong, Anthony," she said. "I do realize what I do. For instance, I am very aware"—she was smiling at him, a brilliant smile that should have warned him but didn't—"of doing this!" Her small foot applied itself with all its might to the viscount's shin.

Startled, he dropped his hands, allowing his horses to break into a gallop. Instantly they were checked, and Chilesworth glared at her. "Here now, Frederica!" he said. "What the devil—" He broke off as he saw her reach down and surreptitiously rub her toes; knowing the thin slippers she wore, he wouldn't be a bit surprised if she had hurt herself more than him, and he grinned. "That just proves my point, doesn't it?" he asked with a smugness that made her long to kick him again.

"I don't know what you mean," Frederica said, staring away from him, out across the park.

"Yes, you do."

Another carriage drove by, and they both smiled at its occupants before Frederica decided the best defense was a strong offense.

"You are being ridiculous, Anthony!" she told him, sitting up very straight in the hopes it would bring her closer to the viscount's imposing height. Disgruntled, she found it did not. "*You* danced twice with Annabella Chittington last night, but *I* am not trying to throw a spoke in *your* wheel!"

"Annabella Chittington is not the same as Baron Barnsley."

"Oh?" Frederica turned a politely inquiring gaze his way, and Chilesworth felt his patience, never held in the firmest of grips, slipping.

"Annabella Chittington is not dangerous."

"Hmmph!" Frederica's small nose was in the air. "She is for persons who need to avoid overdoses of sugar!"

"Frederica!" he said, chastising her. Then his face broke into a big grin. "Why, my dear," he said, "I didn't know you cared!"

Frederica regarded him with suspicion. "What?"

"Admit it!" His grin grew. "You were jealous."

"Jealous!" She gaped at him. "Of *Annabella Chittington?* Whatever for?"

"For me."

"For *you*?" Frederica considered kicking him again and again, but her toes protested. "Of all the—" She clamped her teeth together and her fists were clenched tight as they rode for several moments in silence before Frederica said, her tone devoid of inflection, "If your tastes run to such sweetness, Anthony, I am surprised you did not offer for Annabella ages ago, and save us both all this trouble. Although there are *many* people in the ton who would find it difficult to believe that you could prefer Annabella to, oh, say, half the world, or even . . . me!"

"I did not say I prefer Annabella, Frederica." Chilesworth was calm. "I simply said that she is not dangerous as Baron Barnsley is. You're the one who took us down this garden path."

Frederica's chin rose and she stared straight ahead. They had come to a place in the park where there were no other carriages to be seen, and the viscount pulled his team to a halt. Taking that stubborn little chin in his hand, he turned her face to his as he said, "We could deal better together than this, Frederica."

For a moment she thought he was going to kiss her, and the thought both surprised and—what? She could not decide.

He dropped his hand and shifted back, away from her. "Oblige me in this," he said.

Frederica gave her head a small shake to clear it; the viscount interpreted the movement as a no.

"Do you care so much for him, then, and so little for me?" His voice was harsh.

Frederica blinked. "No," she said. "That is . . ." Anthony was frowning, and she frowned back at him. "I do not consider the baron dangerous, Anthony. He amuses me. He makes me laugh."

The viscount gave an impatient shrug and started his team forward. Frederica put a hand on his shoulder. "Perhaps if you would tell me why you do not wish me to be in his company . . ."

Chilesworth's jaw tightened. "I cannot."

"Oh." Frederica stared at him. "I see."

It was clear from the words that she did not, and Chilesworth said, exasperated, "You do not see, and I cannot tell you, because of a promise given another."

"I see."

It was getting worse and worse, the viscount could tell. "Another woman?"

He nodded.

"I see."

"You do not. Believe me, Frederica, you do not. But I am serious in this. While we are betrothed, have naught to do with Baron Barnsley."

She sniffed. "I have told you I would not wager with him, Anthony, but I see no reason to refrain from being polite to him when we are in company, seeing as how you cannot trust me with your reason!"

He half turned, and for a moment there was a pleading in his eyes. It vanished quickly, and Frederica was left frowning up into a face that could, she saw, be as implacable as his father's. "You will, of course, do as you wish," he said. "But if you wish to oblige me, you will avoid the baron."

By now they had reentered more traveled paths of the park. Frederica, nodding and smiling to her acquaintances, did not answer, but the rigidity of her small back did.

Chilesworth sighed. He was right. She would, of course, do as she wished. Neither of them had any doubt about it.

Chapter
Fourteen

"OH, GEORGE!" HER brother was just coming down the stairs as Frederica entered the mansion, and her happiness at seeing him struck him as excessive. "Just the person with whom I wished to speak! Can you spare me a moment?"

Even as he nodded, her brother was taking in her dress and heightened color. Following her to the library—where, Frederica said, they might be cozy, causing George's suspicions to increase—Frederica's brother said, "Been driving, have you, Freddie?"

"I wish, George," she complained, "that you would remember my name!"

"Frederica," he amended, opening the library door for her and stepping back so she might precede him into the book-lined room where a cheery fire burned on the hearth. Dropping into one of the big leather chairs by the fireplace, Frederica pulled her gloves absently through her fingers and said that yes, she had been driving.

"Oh." George waited. When it seemed he might wait a long time, he tried, "Take your new grays out, did you?"

No, Frederica said, she had not; she had been driving with Anthony in Hyde Park. "And he never even *offered* to let me drive his chestnuts, either!" the lady said, adding that to her long list of viscount grievances.

"Tony never lets any lady drive his horses," George said, excusing him.

His sister looked at him and her back straightened. "I am not just *any* lady, George."

No. Her brother's agreement was silent. She was not.

"Besides"—Frederica pulled her gloves through her fingers again and gazed into the fire—"you let me drive your horses, George, and you know they come to no harm."

"Not as high bred 'uns as Tony's," George said without thinking.

Frederica frowned at him. "Do you think I *couldn't* drive Anthony's chestnuts, George?"

He saw the spark starting at the back of her eyes and disclaimed her question, but her eyelids dropped and he couldn't read the message there. Clearing his throat, he asked if his sister wanted him to speak with Anthony about letting her drive the team.

"I do not!" The reply was vehement, and her eyes were wide open now, so he could read the intensity there. "As if I need you or anyone else to intercede for me with Anthony!"

George's relief was obvious, "Just as well," he said. "Don't think he'd do more than laugh at me if I were to ask him."

Something in his sister's face suggested that was not the most tactful disclosure, either, and George, who usually did better than this in minding his tongue, sighed. "Made a batch of it last night, Freddie," he apologized. "My head isn't working quite right yet. You must forgive me."

"Frederica," corrected the woman by the fire, but it was apparent her heart wasn't in it. She didn't even take the opportunity offered to note that his head was never working quite right.

"Frederica," he echoed, watching her.

She sat in silence for several moments until George, growing more uneasy as time passed, said, "Was there something, Fredd—erica? Because I'm to meet some friends—"

"George," Frederica said, squaring her shoulders as her full violet gaze fixed on his face, "do you know why Anthony holds Baron Barnsley in such dislike?"

Her brother took a step back, and to her surprise his jaw tightened. He hesitated a moment, then nodded.

"Oh, good!" Relieved, Frederica's face was expectant. "Then you can tell me!"

No, her brother said; no, he could not.

Frederica's expectant gaze turned to one of dismay. "What?"

"I cannot tell you, Frederica." George's voice was grave. "It is a matter of honor."

"But, George"—she looked at him, aggrieved—"I have honor too!"

His eyes softened, and his smile was as gentle as his voice. "I know you do, Freddie. But this is not a matter of my honor but the honor of someone else."

"Oh." Frederica thought. "Anthony?"

Her brother nodded. "Anthony and . . . someone else."

"A woman." She bit her lip, and her brother was surprised by the flicker of something—he couldn't be sure what—that passed over her face.

"Why do you say that, Frederica?" he asked.

"Chilesworth said it was a woman."

"Oh." George understood. "So you've already had this conversation with Anthony."

"No! That is, not this conversation . . ." Her voice trailed away as she sighed and returned her gaze to the fire. George came forward and took the chair across from her.

"What is this about, Frederica?" he asked.

"Anthony," she said. "When we were driving this afternoon, he tried to forbid me from dancing or conversing with Baron Barnsley from now on."

George emitted a low whistle. He knew his friend could be foolhardy at times, but he had not expected this. Frederica looked at him.

"He would not tell me why, George."

"*Could* not," her brother said, correcting her. "But it would be a good idea nevertheless. Barnsley can be dangerous, Frederica—more dangerous than you know."

"That is what Anthony said." Frederica was watching him closely. "He said I must trust him on this, George, but he does not trust me enough to tell me why."

"Can you not trust him, Frederica?" her brother asked.

The lady sighed. "It isn't that I don't trust him, George. Actually, after spending my childhood and this last month so much in his company, I suppose I would trust Anthony with just about anyth—" She stopped and shook herself, jerking her gloves through her hands again. "But I don't see it as a question of trust, George."

"You don't?"

His sister's eyes changed from lavender to deep violet. "He tried to *forbid* me, George. Not discuss with me but *forbid* me."

"Ahh."

Frederica's look was one of suspicion. "And what does that mean?"

George smiled. "That Anthony was very foolish. And that you don't like having your will crossed, do you, Freddie?"

Well, no; no, she supposed she didn't, any more than the next person.

Looking at her brother's smiling face, she wasn't about to say so. Instead she said, "I don't like being ordered about without being given reason sufficient for the requested action, George." The words came out quite as lofty as she had hoped, and Frederica was pleased.

"Sometimes, Frederica," her brother said, "the sufficient reason is that you were asked."

Her eyes widened and Frederica bit her lip. "Tell me, George"—she watched his face, as if she were trying to read his thoughts—"if I said to you right now, 'George, never speak with Cassandra Schevington again,' what would you do?"

Her brother started. "But I meet Cassandra everywhere! How could I, without giving offense—"

"Precisely." Frederica was triumphant. Her brother's brow furrowed.

"It is not the same thing, Frederica."

"Why not?"

"Because Anthony has good reason—"

"But I might have good reason to ask you to avoid Cassandra!"

"And that good reason would be . . . ?"

His sister's face was calm. "I cannot tell you, George."

"Ahh." It was a low expulsion of breath, and Frederica nodded.

"What would you do, George?"

Her brother sighed again. "I suppose," he said, the words coming slow, "I would do my best to avoid Cassandra."

"You *would*?"

He nodded.

"Even without my telling you why you should?"

George's head moved slowly up and down. "I have known you all your life, Frederica, and I have known Cassandra only a year. If you felt there was sufficient reason to warn me, I would have to believe in you. Although I might hope that you would see fit, at some later date, to make clear why . . ."

His words trailed off, and Frederica returned her gaze to the fire. "Cassandra Schevington is a pearl beyond price, George," she said, not looking at him. "I wish you well with her."

Her brother colored and was glad his sister's attention

was diverted. "I d-don't know what you mean!" he said, stuttering.

At that Frederica looked up and smiled. "Really, George!" she said.

"I—I—"

Frederica laughed as George ran a nervous hand around his cravat. A thought occurred to him and his hand stilled.

"Freddie," he said, his eyes anxious, "you don't feel for Barnsley as I . . . feel for Miss Schevington . . . ?"

His sister's surprise was so genuine, he need not have worried, and George sat back, relaxed.

"Barnsley?" Frederica said. "Of course not, George! It is just that he can be so amusing. And I see no reason to avoid him because Anthony has taken him in dislike—"

"With cause," her brother said.

"Tell me, George," she coaxed, knowing before she said it that he would not. Her smile disappeared and she sat very still. "I do not like being forbidden something on a whim, George," she said.

"It is not a whim, Frederica."

"And I will not be forbidden by someone who has no right—" She pulled herself up on the words and blushed at her brother's measured look.

"What game are you playing, Frederica?"

She shook her head. "I don't know what you mean, George."

"I mean, what are you up to? What makes you think that your betrothed has no right, unless you do not consider yourself really betrothed? And if that is the case, my dear, you are playing a deep and dangerous game that father is sure to catch you at. If he doesn't smoke it out, you can be sure the Earl of Manningham will!"

Frederica felt her color heighten, and she gazed down at the large emerald stone Anthony had given her two weeks earlier as an engagement present. "But of course I am engaged, George!" she said, holding up her hand to remind him of the ring. "How can you doubt it?"

His expression said that he could doubt it easily, and Frederica chastised herself for her slip of tongue. Trying to recover, she said, "I do not believe that being betrothed gives one person the right to order the other, do you, George?"

Her brother had to admit he did not, but he added, his scrutiny keen, "But surely it does give one the right to . . . request?"

Frederica bit her lip and looked away, even as she nodded. "To . . . request. Yes, George. To request."

He rose and patted her on the shoulder. "I do not believe Anthony has made too many . . . requests, my dear. Has he?"

He was satisfied by the arrested look in the eyes she raised to his. Trying to think, Frederica could not recall one other. Although Chilesworth had had a great deal to say on just about every aspect of her life, he had not tried to direct those aspects. Only this . . .

"You have been a big help to me, George," Frederica said, her gaze once again returning to the fire.

Wanting to say more, her brother decided he had already said enough and walked to the door after dropping a brief kiss in her hair.

"Think carefully about what it is you want, Frederica," he advised her, startling her into turning her face toward him as he opened the door. "Because you just might get it."

Frederica puzzled on that for over an hour after he was gone.

Chapter
Fifteen

FREDERICA WASN'T SURE what she would do the next time she met Baron Barnsley in company, for on one hand she had no intention of letting Viscount Anthony Chilesworth think he—or anyone else, for that matter, but especially *him*!—could dictate to her. On the other hand, she had found, much to her surprise in the past month, that Anthony could be—well, rather nice on occasion, and she had no great desire to cause a severe disagreement with him over matters that meant little to her. Heaven knew there were any number of things causing them minor disagreements, over which they quarreled mightily, without seeking out something major! Plus, in her heart of hearts, Frederica was much more willing to place her dependence on Anthony's and George's assessment of a man than on the unreliable baron's. And while she might feel a little regret parting from Barnsley's wickedly amusing company, there were others who amused her almost as much.

No, the question, she kept telling herself, was one of whether or not she cared to please Anthony in this way. And whether or not she did seemed a great deal to depend on where they were at the moment. Which was why she had been relieved to hear, at the Schevingtons' select musicale the evening after her discussion with the viscount, that Baron Barnsley had been called out of town unexpectedly by the ill health of an uncle on whose expectations the baron had lived for years. That the news had made Anthony look like a cat in the cream pot had been enough to make her wish the baron were there right then, so she could flirt outrageously with him. But as the night progressed, with one long musical piece following another, Frederica had been quite in charity with her betrothed, who had had the foresight to find them seats at the back of the room and who had no pangs of conscience, after the first hour, in suggesting that they slip out and repair to Frederica's for a game of chess. It was in the library, engrossed in the game, where Frederica's parents found them when they returned from the musicale a full two hours later, Frederica's father highly indignant that they had escaped without him.

Her father's face had made her laugh, but Frederica was not laughing this night as she sat, caught in a corner of the Barrington's ballroom by Lord Brumley, who had been prosing on for some forty minutes about his year-long experience in Brazil. Frederica, who felt he was telling the story of the entire year minute by minute, asked desperately if he would not like to dance.

Brumley gazed out at the whirling couples, his placid face containing an expression of infinite superiority as he said that he did not waltz.

"You do not?" Frederica saw Geoffrey Kingston enter the ballroom door and tried unsuccessfully to catch his eye. Geoffrey was one of her oldest friends, and a beautiful dancer.

"No." Lord Brumley slewed his portly body more fully toward her, putting an end to the desperate hand signals she'd been making behind his back in the hopes of attracting Geoffrey. "I cannot think it is good for the kingdom."

Frederica blinked. "I . . . beg your pardon?" she asked. She was sure she had not heard right.

Lord Brumley favored Frederica with one of his superior smiles. "I am sure it is not a thought with which you have bothered your pretty little head, Lady Frederica," he said, "for I know ladies do dearly love frivolous things. And the waltz, you must admit, is decidedly frivolous." He paused and pursed his lips together. "Even, I think, fast."

Frederica could think for once of nothing to say, which was just as well, and she continued to stare at him. Lord Brumley took her shock for admiration and preened. "Of course," he told her, capturing one of the hands that lay listless in her lap, "you must not think I am averse to granting ladies others treats dear to their hearts." He laughed. "I daresay that were I to be . . . oh, shall we say, attached, to a lady, I would be found to be quite generous, indeed."

That was accompanied by such an arch look that Frederica could only goggle at him further. Feeling that something was expected of her, she managed a weak, "You would?"

Lord Brumley nodded, and his hold on her hand tightened. "I would," he said. "Lady Frederica, I wonder—"

He got no further, for they were interrupted by Viscount Chilesworth, who dropped a friendly hand on Brumley's shoulder and said, his eyes alight, "So! This is where you are hiding yourself, Frederica! We have almost missed our waltz, you know."

Never had his betrothed appeared so glad to see him, rising with alacrity to take his arm. "Anthony!" she said, beaming. She turned toward her former companion, who appeared crestfallen at her defection. "Look, Lord Brumley! It's Chilesworth! Come to dance!"

Lord Brumley rose and smiled at them both. "I must thank you, Lady Frederica," he said, "for the pleasure of your company. It is not every day I find a woman with your good sense who is so interested in my adventures in Brazil."

Frederica's face was indignant and she would have told

anyone less self-involved than Lord Brumley that she had been far from interested in his tales. Chilesworth, watching her, had to bite back his laughter. That was effectively erased from his face a moment later, however, as Lord Brumley, about to take his leave, said, "And I must thank you, too, Chilesworth, for telling me of Lady Frederica's great interest in Brazil."

Brumley had barely turned his back when Frederica dropped her fiancé's arm as if burned by it. She glared up at him, her wide eyes sparking fire. "You!" she breathed.

The viscount made a deft catch as she threw her fan at him, then handed it back to her as another couple came to occupy the bench Frederica had so gratefully vacated moments earlier. "Yours, my dear," the viscount said, giving her the fan as he took her elbow to move her away from the new arrivals. Not waiting for her to renew her attack, he swept her out onto the floor as another waltz started.

"Of all the despicable—" Frederica said.

The viscount favored her with a wide smile. "Your mother is watching," he told her.

Frederica smiled, too, all the time hissing at him every derogatory term that came to her mind. The viscount grinned.

"How could you?" she ended as they twirled about the room.

Try as he might, Chilesworth could not appear innocent as he said, his tone as neutral as possible, that he had just been trying to help her with her search for a suitable mate, and knowing of her great interest in Brazil . . .

"My only great interest in Brazil," Frederica said, fired up now, "is seeing you there, my lord!"

"Why, Frederica." He gave her a tender look that she had no trouble interpreting as meant for the benefit of his and her parents, who were in her range of vision as she and Anthony danced by. "Am I really one of your great interests?!"

"You know very well what I meant!" Frederica said, her eyes once again stormy now that her parents and Anthony's no longer could see her face.

The dance was ending, but Anthony did not relinquish his hold on her hand. Instead he pulled her with him to a small bench by one of the long, open windows that led out onto the balcony. Through the opening Frederica could see a starlit sky, and she sighed as she applied her fan to her hot face.

"So," Anthony said, not looking at her as the orchestra struck up another dance, "you don't want Brumley, then, I take it?" Her glare made her answer clear. "He informed me at the club the other day that he had been about to ask for your hand—having decided, in ways inscrutable to me, that the two of you would suit admirably—when he heard through the grapevine of our engagement."

"As if I would marry him—even to escape you!" Frederica sat up straight, her eyes flashing.

"In that case—" The viscount took her hand and pulled her to her feet and out onto the balcony.

"Anthony . . ." she began. He stopped long enough to nod toward where the gentleman in question was making his purposeful if ponderous way across the floor toward them.

"Unless I very much miss my guess," the viscount told her, "he is on his way to ask you to dance."

"Oh, no!" Frederica groaned. "Of course! It *is* a country dance."

Chilesworth had started forward again, but at that he stopped to ask what that had to do with anything.

"Lord Brumley," Frederica informed him, "does not waltz."

"What?"

She moved ahead of the viscount now, to lose herself in the shadows before Lord Brumley could reach the bench where he'd last seen her, only to find her gone and look about for her. "He finds it frivolous. And he worries that it will destroy the kingdom."

"What?" Anthony's startled exclamation was loud and she shushed him immediately.

"Do be quiet, Anthony!" she said. "This is all your fault, after all!"

Chilesworth disclaimed that, saying he rather thought Brumley's parents must take the responsibility for having produces such a clod-pate. Frederica giggled as she sank down onto a bench in the shadows of the high hedge that ran through the garden. The viscount slipped with careless grace onto the bench beside her.

"So, Brumley is out," Chilesworth said, picking up a stick from the grass and breaking it into small pieces. An emphatic Frederica said that he was.

"He is a pattern card of all that is respectable," Anthony reminded her. "Not a breath of scandal attaches to his name."

Frederica snorted. "Scandal would be bored to tears within moments of his acquaintance! Of course it doesn't attach itself to him!"

Chilesworth laughed. "Well," he said, "I saw you flirting with young Byrington quite desperately several nights past. Does he measure up?"

A flushing Frederica said she was surprised he had noticed, when he had been devoting his full attention—and perhaps a little more—to the dashing Widow Smythely. And, she added, not able to see his face in the darkness, *she*, for one, did not *flirt desperately*. Unlike others she could name.

"So," Chilesworth said, "does that mean Byrington is a possibility, then?"

Frederica shook her head in frustration. "No," she said, "I am afraid he is not, Anthony. I really did think he might be, because he is so pleasant to look at, after all, and a wonderful dancer, but . . . he doesn't play chess. Or whist."

The viscount suggested that the man might learn. Frederica shook her head again.

"He does not care to," she said. "I asked him. And his sister tells me that when they are in the country, he falls asleep each night before the fire and . . . he *snores*!"

"Oh! Well!" There was a teasing note in Chilesworth's voice that made her flush. "Snoring! We can't have that!"

He thought a moment, then asked, "Tell me, Freddie, if I snored . . ."

He let the words drift off, and there was tartness in the lady's voice when she said it didn't matter because she wasn't considering him, anyway.

The viscount tossed the last of the stick he'd been breaking away and dusted his hands with his handkerchief. "So," he said, "have you someone else in mind?"

"I was thinking that Johnathan Waddington has always been a pleasant dance partner—"

The viscount snorted. "That fop!"

"Just because a man cares about his appearance—"

Chilesworth snorted again. "It would never do, my dear," he told her. "Waddington will never choose a bride better-looking than himself."

"Hmmph!" They sat in silence for several moments, Frederica miffed with his assessment of her possible partners. It seemed as if each time she suggested someone, Anthony had something to say to his disparagement. In the past few weeks he had almost scared young Mr. Mattington away from approaching her anytime Chilesworth was in the room. Frederica sighed and said, "What about you?"

"What?" Anthony appeared startled, and she wished she could read his face in the darkness.

"Have you found anyone yet who arouses your interest?" She felt more than saw his quick grin, and wished she had chosen her words with more care.

"Oh, many!" The viscount's voice was cheerful. "But none that prompts me to marriage!"

"I do not believe you are trying, Anthony!" she complained. "Which is odd, because in the past I have always found you *terribly* trying!"

The viscount grinned. "I told you before, Freddie, marriage is not something I'm anxious to try!" Through the open doors they could hear that the country dance had ended, and already the orchestra was starting another song. It was a waltz, and Chilesworth rose, holding a hand down to her.

"Come, Frederica," he said, mindful that she had just corrected him when he used her childhood name—as she always did and which he almost always ignored. "Let us see if King George's England can withstand one more waltz!"

The lady acquiesced and soon they were floating to the music. She sighed, the sound a bit regretful. It was too bad, she thought, considering their circumstances, that Anthony should be such a very good dancer.

Chapter
Sixteen

"YOU KNOW, FREDERICA," the Countess of Forkham said several weeks later as she and her daughter sat in the Forkham carriage on their way to visit the countess's favorite milliner, "I have been remiss about this, but there . . . we have all of us been so busy this season, and your father and I thought it best if you and Anthony had some time, although maybe that wasn't best . . ."

Her words trailed off, leaving her daughter still unenlightened as to what Lady Forkham felt she had been remiss about. Frederica smiled at her mother and at the abstracted frown puckering her lovely forehead. Privately Frederica wished she could look just like the countess when she reached her mother's age.

"Mama," Frederica said teasingly, "you are losing yourself in your sentences again."

She had to say it twice, for it was apparent the countess was deeply concerned with what was on her mind and was lost in her thoughts as well as in her sentences.

"Oh, am I?" Lady Forkham replied, when Frederica's words at last penetrated. "Well, there! If that isn't just like me."

Yes, thought Frederica, it is. She smiled again when it

seemed her mother thought she now had explained. "Yes, Mama?" she questioned.

The countess looked at her, surprised. "Yes?" The surprised changed to happiness. "Oh, Frederica!" she cried, capturing and clasping one of her daughter's hands in delight. "If only I'd known it would be this easy! I told your father I thought it most cowardly of him to make me be the one to speak with you about it, but there— It hasn't gone so badly, has it? You said yes with no hesitation, and . . . and . . . " She faltered as she peered into her daughter's face. "That is . . ."

Frederica withdrew her hand, her brow starting to furrow. Although she did not yet know what her mother was talking about, she was, judging from her mother's words just now, pretty sure she was not going to like it.

"Mama," Frederica said, "you still have not told me what you are talking about."

"I . . . I haven't?" her mother said. Dismay spread across her face.

"No, Mama!"

"No, Mama!" The countess mourned. "I very much feared that would be your more likely response—"

"Mama!" Frederica was both amused and vexed. "*What on earth are you talking about?*"

"Bride clothes," the countess said. She sat back to give careful consideration to Frederica's reaction to this pronouncement.

"Bride—" Frederica repeated the word blankly. When its meaning penetrated her full consciousness, two bright spots burned in her cheeks and her startled eyes flew to her mother's. After a moment she managed a shaky laugh. "Bride clothes, Mama! Really! We have plenty of time!"

"But that is just it, Frederica," the countess said. "Although you and Anthony are known to be engaged—in a little less than a month we will have your engagement ball at Forkham mansion—people are beginning to ask when the wedding is to be, and as far as I know, you have not yet set a date. . . ." The countess's words trailed off as she gave her daughter a hopeful look. "You haven't set a date yet, have you, dear?"

At the quick shake of Frederica's head the countess sighed. "Frederica, my dear." She put a hand on her daughter's knee and gazed intently into her face. "You *are* planning to marry, are you not?"

Frederica nodded, salving her conscience that that was, at least, true. She *did* plan to marry. She just did not plan to marry the person her mother now thought she would.

"Then you must set a date."

Frederica searched her mind for a reason why she could not do so immediately; happily, a legitimate one was at hand.

"But, Mama," she protested, "as you know, Anthony has posted down to Chilesworth Manor for several days, and I cannot set a date without him!"

No, the countess agreed, she could not. But just when Frederica was feeling relieved, Lady Forkham added, "But when he comes back, Frederica, the two of you must make all due haste to do so. Naturally you will want to consult your father and me, and George, and Anthony's parents—and probably his Cousin Eliza, for she has always been the closest thing Anthony has to a sister, and she will have to come to town—she hardly ever comes to London, you know! In fact, you might wish to ask her to be a bridesmaid, Frederica; that would be a lovely thing to do for Anthony— As to dates that will work well for us—"

The countess was ticking these things off on her fingers as she thought of them, but she stopped when it seemed her daughter was not paying attention. "Frederica?" she questioned.

Frederica's eyes were opened wide. "B-b-bridesmaid?" It was clear that that was the last word her daughter had heard.

The countess's trilling laugh filled the carriage. "But of course, my love! You must think who else you would like to have, not that you must ask Eliza, of course, but I am sure Anthony and his parents would be pleased, and—"

"Mama," Frederica said, interrupting, "have I *met* Anthony's Cousin Eliza?"

The countess laughed again. "But of course, my dear!" she said. "Don't you remember? I believe it was the summer you were twelve and Anthony and his parents came to Farthingham Hall to visit. Eliza came with them. She was a year or two older than Anthony and quite a young lady—the prettiest thing. Don't you remember how she went fishing with you? She had such merry brown eyes and the happiest laugh."

Frederica nodded. She did remember. "I thought she was beautiful," she said, "and not at all high in the instep. She played with me without making me feel that I was a child and she a grown-up doing me a favor. She was the one who thought of the trick we played on Anthony and George—"

Frederica stopped herself, knowing that the intervening years would not stop her mother from calling down a rebuke upon her head for that trick that had served both of the young men well but which her mother might not see in quite that light. Instead she changed the subject. "Now that you speak of her, Mama, I remember a year later hearing George and Anthony talk about how Eliza was the toast of the town! Why have I never met her here since my coming out?"

The countess repeated her statement that Eliza seldom came to London. There was something about the way her mother looked out the window as she said it that made Frederica suspicious.

"Why, Mama?"

The countess turned back toward her daughter. "Well, dear," she said, "Eliza married that nice Mr. Plumton, and they went to live on his estate in Yorkshire. She has several children now, and Anthony's mother says she is quite content to remain in Yorkshire, preferring not to leave the children to another's care or drag them along to the city, where she might not be able to spend as much time as she likes with them during a season."

Frederica had a vague memory of the laughing Eliza, her eyes sparkling, confiding how much she was looking forward to her first season. It was hard to believe the lady had eschewed town life of her own accord. A thought struck her. "Mama," she demanded, "does her husband prevent her from attending the season?"

The countess's look of astonishment was real. "Mr. Plumton?" she said. "Oh, my dear, no! He truly is the kindest, gentlest man—and so in love with his wife! From the first time he saw her, I understand! No, the Countess of Manningham tells me that more than once he has urged Eliza to come to town with him, but she prefers not to."

"Mr. Plumton?" Frederica's forehead furrowed further. "I do not believe I have met a Mr. Plumton."

No, the countess said, she probably had not; he did not visit the metropolis often, since Eliza did not care to come, and when he was in London, he did not choose to go about in society much without his wife, preferring to attend a few of those dreary societies men such as Frederica's father and the Earl of Manningham were so addicted to, and catching up with old friends.

Frederica smiled to hear the intellectual discussion group her father belonged to described as a "dreary society" but persisted in trying to learn more about Eliza. There was something in what her mother said—or didn't say—that made her sense a mystery there.

"Mama," Frederica said, "did something happen in Eliza's first season?"

The countess started, and her eyes opened wide. She bit her lip, then laughed. "Why, yes, dearest," she said. "She married Mr. Plumton!"

Frederica shook her head. "No, Mama," she insisted. "I mean something else."

The countess's eyes opened wider, a movement that gave lie to her next words. "Why, Frederica," Lady Forkham said, slipping farther back into her corner. "I don't know what you mean!" Then, before her daughter could say more, she added, "Now, about those bride clothes . . ."

So intent was her mother on making up for what she persisted in calling lost time that when they left the milliner's, Frederica possessed three more hats than she had going in, and one blue silk parasol with a darker blue fringe that exactly matched the ruched silk lining of her second new bonnet, trimmed with a feather that curled charmingly over her left ear and loops of ribbon that matched the ruched lining. The hat was, the countess admitted, shockingly dear, but since it *was* for Frederica's bride clothes and they were both agreed that it would look so charming with Frederica's new blue velvet pelisse, delivered just last week . . .

Frederica, not at all keen on this attention to a wardrobe for her wedding, suggested they return home, but the countess, her shopping blood aroused, directed the coachman to drive them to the shop of Madame Chautinand, a modiste known almost as much for her genius with dress designs as for her exorbitant fees.

"After all, dearest," the countess said when Frederica protested, "it is not quite a month to our ball, and I would wager that you have not yet given one thought to what you are to wear for that special occasion." Her daughter's flush made her cluck. "Really, Frederica! It is your night to shine, and you have not even thought of it—"

"I thought I would wear my green silk," her daughter mumbled. The countess shook her head.

"Certainly not," Lady Forkham said. "You have worn that dress several times now, and I won't have people saying that my daughter could not even have something new for her betrothal ball! Besides"—the countess's eyes crinkled as they stopped in front of the modiste's shop, and a footman sprang down to open the carriage door for them—"I want something new myself!"

Once inside, the countess's desire to provide them both with something new, out of the ordinary, and—the thought made Madame Chautinand's eyes brighten, although she kept that to herself—no doubt costly, was met with enthusiasm by the modiste. Lady Forkham and her oh so lovely daughter had long been two of Madame Chautinand's favorite clients, for not only did they both set off her creations to perfection, but also the countess had an excellent fashion sense and was aware of every new design—every new nuance—to be found in *La Belle Assemblée*. Plus, in Madame Chautinand's opinion, the value of these clients was heightened by the ready and prompt manner in which the earl paid every one of the very tasteful—and very expensive—bills Madame Chautinand sent his way.

Since they were the only customers in her shop at the time, Madame Chautinand was able to give them her undivided attention—attention that grew even more undivided as she heard the countess's plans for their ball toilettes. It was all Madame Chautinand could do to keep from rubbing her hands together in anticipation.

Frederica was to have a gown of gauze over satin, the satin a periwinkle blue and the gauze one that Madame Chautinand, after a snap of her fingers, had disappeared into a storeroom to find, emerging perhaps ten minutes later carrying the bolt of material with a reverence Frederica had never before seen. It was a lighter shade of blue, embroidered with tiny flowers of silvery silk thread. Madame Chautinand told them almost in a whisper that she had guarded it for two years, saving it for just the right creation. It would, she said, with the small seed pearls arranged by an expert—herself—be perfect for Frederica's gown's small puffed sleeves. The gauze—its embroidery so fine, it appeared almost fairylike—would be repeated on the skirt of her high-wasited gown. Looking down as the fabric was pinned about her, Frederica felt as if she wore a garden more exquisite than any she had ever seen.

"Mama . . ." she began, raising her eyes to her mother's in wonder.

The countess smiled. "You will be beautiful, my darling," Lady Forkham said, her face beaming with pride. Madame Chautinand made haste to agree, and her own eyes misted. This would be a dress guaranteed to send fifty anxious mamas to her shop the day after the Forkham ball, each eager to find such a gown for her own daughter of marriageable age.

Frederica fingered the material. "I've never seen anything so beautiful!" she said. Madame Chautinand promised a shawl of the gauze to drape just so over Frederica's elbows when she walked and danced and stood to receive her guests.

"You will be *magnifique*!" Madame Chautinand kissed her fingers. "And I would suggest, if you will permit, that you wear your hair simply, perhaps with a blue flower placed so." Madame Chautinand demonstrated. "And, of course, long gloves, and satin slippers to match the undershirt." She looked to the countess for confirmation, and Lady Forkham nodded.

"And, of course, your sapphire necklace, my dear, with the matching bracelet," the countess said.

"Sapphires!" Madame Chautinand gave her enthusiastic approval. "But of course!" Again her eyes misted at the picture presented. "Your gown will be my crowning achievement, mademoiselle! People will talk of it for days—weeks—perhaps forever!" She kissed her fingers again, almost carried away by the vision. Then her practical nature returned.

"And for madame?" she said.

The countess smiled. "For madame," Lady Forkham said, "a gown of"—she eyed her daughter critically—"green," she decided. "Something to complement Frederica's blue." Madame Chautinand had just the thing, she assured the countess, and sent two of her assistants flying to find it. They returned with a green silk, shot through with gold.

Lucinda nodded. "Over a white satin slip, I think," the countess said, thinking aloud. Madame Chautinand's head bobbed up and down in approval. "I shall wear the diamonds your father gave me for our last anniversary, my dear," Lady Forkham continued to Frederica, "and the emerald comb that was your grandmama's in my hair."

"You will be beautiful, Mama," Frederica said. Madame Chautinand nodded; she had not had a better day in some time.

The countess's smile was placid. "I believe," she said, thinking of her husband and the way his eyes lit up when he saw her in something he particularly liked, "that I will do."

On their way home Frederica was relieved to realize that plans for their ball gowns had, at least for the moment, driven the thought of more bride clothes from her mother's mind. Frederica crossed her fingers and hoped that this would be more than temporary.

Chapter
Seventeen

VISCOUNT CHILESWORTH ARRIVED at his London town house one day earlier than expected. He was cold, he was wet—the night being a rainy one, and he having chosen to drive himself and his phaeton back to town—and he was tired. The viscount's mood was not a pleasant one, and he wanted nothing more than a good supper and his bed.

His temper was not improved to find, when he arrived unannounced at his home, that neither his butler nor his chef awaited him, both having decided to take advantage of one last free night to enjoy themselves before their employer returned.

The second footman, answering the door, was put out of countenance by his lordship's unsmiling face—something the viscount's staff seldom saw, for Chilesworth usually was an even-tempered young man where they were concerned, fair and not given to whims and starts. The footman started to sputter.

His sputtering increased when he had to tell his lordship that the chef was gone, and he nearly fainted when the viscount said that well, then, the cook's helper could throw something together for him. The footman, picturing the new cook's helper's face upon delivery of that careless order, paled.

"Yes, your lordship. I'm sure, your lordship," the footman said, receiving the viscount's dripping coat and hat. "That is, the cook's helper is new, my lordship, and—"

The viscount, who had not been "his lordshipped" so many times in years, frowned and reached for the mail awaiting him on the small table in his foyer. "Eggs," he said.

The footman goggled at him. "Eggs, your lordship?" the man repeated, as if he'd never heard of them.

"Eggs," the viscount said. "Have the fellow scramble me some eggs. And ham. There is surely a ham around here someplace?"

Chilesworth's inquiring and still frowning gaze had transferred itself from his mail to the footman and that poor fellow, afraid of what his idol, Mr. Simmons, the viscount's lofty butler, would tell him he should have done, gulped and nodded. Stiles didn't know if there was a ham about the house, but if there wasn't, he was willing to dash out through the rain to find one, although where he was to do so at this time of night . . .

The footman's head moved up and down. "Yes, your lordship," he agreed, and started toward the back stairs to tell the cook's helper that his chance to shine—or to fall on his face and be ruined forever in his chosen profession—was at hand.

He was stopped when Chilesworth, his attention returned to his mail, added, "And brandy."

"Brandy, your lordship?" The footman could not stop his voice from rising. "In the *eggs*?"

The man's consternation was heard inside the fog of abstraction surrounding Chilesworth, and the viscount looked up. "What?" Anthony said.

Stiles, assuming a wooden tone that accented rather than hid his desperation, said, "Were you wanting the brandy in your eggs, my lord? Or"—another thought occurred to him and his tone grew more hopeful—"maybe as a sauce, on the ham?"

The man's dismay was such that when the source of it occurred to the viscount, he was hard put not to laugh. Chilesworth's face lightened, and he said, each word succinct, "I am wanting the brandy in the library. In a decanter. With a glass."

"Oh." The footman, realizing his mistake, blushed bright red and stuttered, "Of course, m-my lord. At once!"

"At once," the viscount agreed, and strolled into the library with his correspondence to await his servant. He was greeted there by the aging spaniel who always kept guard over the library fire in Anthony's absence. The dog, seeing him, ambled over to the viscount's side and put one polite paw on his boot.

"Hello, old boy," Chilesworth said, and bent to rub the animal's ears in that special spot that always made the dog heave a blissful sigh.

That done, Chilesworth crossed to his favorite chair by the fire and sat down, sorting quickly through the letters in his hand. The contented spaniel sank down beside him, resting his chin on the viscount's crossed ankles.

Anthony was midway through the pile of letters, bills, and notes, having mentally consigned most of them to the fire, when he came upon one written in a feminine hand. Turning it over, he found it bore all the appearances of having been hand-delivered.

"Hmm," he said to the dog, who raised his head in question as the viscount broke the missive's seal. The message inside was brief.

Chilesworth,
The Case is *desperate*. Come at once!
        Frederica.

The viscount frowned and rose, to the spaniel's discomfort. "I'm sorry, old friend," he said, looking down at the sorrowful eyes raised to his own, "but a lady in distress awaits me."

The dog seemed not to think that any excuse, and turned its back on Anthony as it moved closer to the fire. Chilesworth grinned as the footman came through the door, bearing his lordship's best brandy.

"Stiles," he said abruptly, "I am going out."

"You are, my lord?" the footman said, coming close to dropping the tray. He thought of the almost tearful cook's assistant, laboring below in the kitchen and wondering why he'd ever left Kent. "After your eggs and ham, would that be, my lord?"

"No," the viscount said, "that would be before." He would eat upon his return.

The wooden look returned to the footman's face. He did not want to tell the cook's helper he was expected to keep eggs warm for an undisclosed amount of time.

"And I will need a bath," Chilesworth said. "See to it immediately."

"A bath."

"And lay out my blue coat with all that's appropriate, Stiles. Greeves follows me with my luggage, and I don't expect the carriage for some hours yet."

"M-m-*me*, my lord?" the footman squeaked. He was grateful he had set the tray down moments earlier or he was sure that this time he *would* have dropped it. The poor man looked so terrified at even *attempting* the most rudimentary of Mr. Greeve's, his lordship's inestimable valet's, duties that the viscount relented.

"Oh, very well," Chilesworth said, waving him away. "I shall see to my clothing myself. But the bath—"

"Immediately, my lord!" the footman said, and fled.

By the time the viscount had bathed, shaved, and dressed himself, it was after eleven P.M. He hoped that this night

Frederica had not chosen to amuse herself at Almack's, for if she had, he knew he could not get in. The doors to that august institution closed at eleven, and not even the regent himself was allowed admittance thereafter.

Of course, if something was as desperate as her note suggested . . . For some inexplicable reason his eyes went hard and his throat tightened at the thought. *What could it be? An illness in her family? Was she ill or in trouble?*

His jaw clenched and he gripped his cane harder—she might be expected to await him at her home. Experience, however, had taught him that Frederica seldom did the expected, so he did not place much reliance on finding her at this time of night in the midst of the season at the Forkham mansion. Still, he would need to go there to determine her location.

Chilesworth plunged out into the night, holding his hat against the onslaught of rain and wind. He had difficulty locating a hack, cursing himself for not sending his carriage with his valet and luggage back a day before he'd left Chilesworth Manor. But how could he have known that it would rain, or that Fredrica might need—demand—his immediate presence with her talk of a desperate case?

It was just like her, he decided as he at last found and hurried into a far from prepossessing hack, to send him notes he'd receive on a cold, rainy night. Did she ever ask him to come on a sunny day? Not she! Or on an evening when the breezes blew gently and the stars shone overhead? Oh, no!

He continued on in that vein until the hack pulled up outside the Forkham mansion. Snapping at the driver to wait, he hurried up the steps and pounded on the door. A few moments later he was admitted by a startled Higgins, who looked at the raindrops glistening on his coat and said, stuttering, "My-m lord!"

The butler recovered much more smoothly than the viscount's own inexperienced footman and changed that to

"My Lord Chilesworth! What a pleasure to see you! We had understood that you would not be returning to the city until tomorrow at the earliest."

"Yes, yes." The viscount shrugged the polite conversation away. "I'm back early, as you can see. Where is Frederica?"

Higgins said the lady was out, and would be so sorry to have missed him.

"Ha!" said the viscount. "If that were so, she could have waited, couldn't she?"

Chilesworth looked so fierce that Higgins coughed before making the cautious suggestion that the lady had not known her betrothed would be returning to town early and coming to call.

"Where's George?" the viscount demanded.

Higgins regretted to inform him that Lady Frederica's brother also was not at home.

"Yes, well . . ." Chilesworth's stomach rumbled, and he scowled. "I expected as much." He stood brooding for several moments as Higgins gave a delicate sniff in the direction of the viscount's mouth to ascertain if the gentleman was, to put it tactfully, a trifle above par. Smelling no alcohol, he said that he would be very happy to take any message the viscount might care to leave.

"Message?" That brought Chilesworth out of his brown study. "Oho! Messages, is it? I think we've had enough of messages this night!" The butler, who did not understand him, agreed, waiting.

"Where have they gone?" the viscount demanded.

Higgins said he believed the viscount's friend, George, was engaged with a group of friends at Cribb's Parlor.

"Not George!" Chilesworth shrugged away his friend's presence with impatience. "Frederica!"

"My Lady Frederica has accompanied the earl and the countess to Manfield House, my lord," Higgins said. "The

Earl and Countess of Manfield are, as I am sure you, a leader of the ton, would know, giving a ball."

"Manfield House?" Chilesworth frowned. Yes, he remembered; he'd declined the invitation, believing he would still be out of town. "I imagine half the world is there!"

"Oh, yes, my lord!" Higgins agreed. The Earl and Countess of Manfield were among the town's most popular hosts and hostesses.

"A crush!" Anthony grabbed the hat he had allowed Higgins to remove and hold tenderly, and crammed it back onto his head. His stomach growled again. "It needed only that!"

Chapter
Eighteen

FREDERICA WAS ENJOYING herself. Her eyes sparkled and she laughed often as she passed from partner to partner through the string of dances played by the excellent orchestra engaged by Manfield and his lady.

Mr. Mattington had had the courage to ask her for not one but two dances, since Chilesworth wasn't nearby to frown him down. The young man's eyes had shone as he dared compliment her on her appearance, his "Lady Frederica, you are in such looks tonight! But then, you always are!" uttered in such heartfelt tones that she was quite touched. She never, she realized, heard such words from Chilesworth. The viscount was much more likely to tell her she had a curl out of place, or that he didn't like her fan, or that yellow did not become her.

A short time ago, after their second dance, Mr. Mattington had escorted her to the bench on which she now sat fanning herself, and had gone off in search of a glass of champagne. When someone touched her shoulder, she expected it to be he and turned, smiling. Her smile faded as she realized the face looking down at hers was not the admiring one of Mr. Mattington, but Baron Barnsley's far more cynical one.

"Lady Frederica," the baron said. He gave a slight bow and sank down onto the bench beside her, taking her fan from her unresisting hands and beginning to apply it gently for her. "A sad crush, is it not?"

His eyes roved over the press of people crowding the Manfield House ballroom, then returned to her. "But what is this?" the baron chided. "You do not look happy to see me!"

It was Frederica's cross thought that it was deucedly hard to look what one was not. Realizing the phrase was Anthony's, she colored. The baron, misunderstanding, paused in fanning her.

"I see." He snapped the fan together and handed it back to her. "Your fiancé has commanded you not to talk with the big bad baron, I suppose."

The words were said with such mockery that Frederica fired up at once. "Anthony does not command, my lord," she said. "No man commands me."

The baron's eyebrow rose in obvious disbelief and Frederica's color grew. "It is just that I was surprised to see you, that is all. I understood you had gone into the country."

The baron made his disbelief known even as he forbore to press her further. "I had," he said. "My uncle was ill."

Frederica applied her fan to her heated cheeks. "I trust he is recovered now," she said.

"Yes, rot him" was the undutiful nephew's reply. "He's likely to live another twenty years!"

Frederica's tone was austere as she said that must make him very happy.

The baron grinned. "Oh, definitely, my lady," he said. "I am delighted to know that I will not have one farthing of that blasted fortune he guards so prodigiously. Who in my circumstances would not be?"

Frederica did not know where to look, for this was the first time she had heard the baron speak so plainly or so bitterly of his circumstances. She had heard, of course, town gossip that said he was living upon his expectations, and that if his uncle did not die soon, he would find himself rolled up. That was why, some whispered, his taste ran to wealthy heiresses and why careful parents kept their daughters away from the wicked baron."

In spite of the heat, Frederica shivered, and Baron Barnsley regarded her closely. "What is it, Lady Frederica?"

"Nothing," she lied, and saw his lips twist into the semblance of a smile. She could not decide if it mocked him or her.

"We used to deal better together than this," he said, his eyes again roving the crowd. "In fact, at one time I thought we might deal very well."

"I don't know what you mean—" she began, then stopped when she felt him stiffen. She heard the soft "tsa, tsa" sound of a fencer issue from his lips, and was looking at him in surprise wondering what had prompted it, when he rose and took her hand in an abrupt hold.

"Dance with me, Lady Frederica," he said.

She protested that she was awaiting her escort, but he brushed the words aside, pulling her to her feet and into the waltzing crowd.

"Baron Barnsley!" Frederica said.

He smiled down at her, an intimate, sensual smile she had never seen before. She caught her breath and thought that there might be good reason to give credence to the warnings of both George and Anthony.

"Do you know that you are quite lovely, Lady Frederica?" he murmured into her ear. She gazed at him in anger.

"Do you know that I do not care to dance with you, Baron Barnsley?" she replied.

He smiled again. "Chilesworth did warn you about me, didn't he?"

Frederica bit her lip and looked away.

The baron nodded, satisfied. "And did he tell you why?"

The lady looked quickly back, her eyes curious. "No," she said. "Will you?"

"No, my dear." He breathed more than said the words in her ear, pulling her closer. "I will not."

Frederica pushed back, trying to put a proper distance between them. "Baron Barnsley," she said, "I wish to stop dancing. Now."

He smiled. "Then isn't it fortunate that the music is ending?" he asked as he brought them to a halt.

Frederica blinked and looked around. For several minutes she had not heard music. "That was badly done of you, sir," she said, stepping away from him. "I do not know why you did it, but—" She felt a firm grip on her upper arm and turned. In seconds she knew why the baron had swept her onto the floor, and why he had made the "tsa, tsa" sound, and she turned a look of searing reproach upon him as she said "Anthony!" in such surprised tones that the viscount's frown, already prominent, deepened.

"Frederica," Chilesworth replied. He was glaring at the baron, and unconsciously his grip on her arm tightened.

"I did not know you had returned to London!" She was rattling on, trying to move him away from Barnsley, but she found that those were an unfortunate choice of words. As soon as she uttered them, the viscount focused on her face.

"Obviously not," he said.

Finding that unfair, Frederica protested, "Now just a moment, Anthony, you misunderstand—"

"Do I, Frederica?" he asked. "Do I?"

The baron, watching them, grinned. "If you will excuse me," he said to the viscount, and moved as if to take Frederica's arm. "This is our dance."

"It is not!" The words came from two sets of mouths, and Chilesworth and Frederica stared at each other for a moment. The frown on the viscount's forehead started to lessen.

"It isn't?" he demanded.

"Certainly not!" Frederica said. "I did not care to dance with Baron Barnsley the last dance, and I have no *intention* of dancing with him for this one!"

"Then dance with me." Chilesworth's hand moved from her arm to her back, and the calm assurance with which he maneuvered her onto the dance floor made her angry.

"I am engaged," she said through clenched teeth as she spotted Mr. Mattington, a glass of champagne in his hand as he stood, uncertain what to do, a few steps away, "to dance with Mr. Mattington there." A challenging gleam grew in her eye. "For the *third* time this evening."

"Mattington?" Chilesworth looked around, and at sight of the young man coming forward at mention of his name his frown disappeared completely.

"My lord," Mr. Mattington began, nervous, then stopped, surprised, as the viscount took the glass of champagne he held and gulped it.

"Thank you, Mattington," Chilesworth said, moving Frederica forward with one hand on her back and the other holding tight to her resisting fingers. "Most kind of you. I was quite thirsty!"

Frederica saw her bewildered suitor's face flash by, as well as the reluctantly appreciative grin of the baron, and glared up at the viscount. "That was my champagne!" she said.

"It was good," the viscount replied.

"And I do not wish to dance with you any more than I wished to dance with Baron Barnsley!"

"Then why were you dancing with him?" Chilesworth was staring over her head, and Frederica, incensed, said it was for much the same reason she now was dancing with him: She had been forced into it.

Anthony stopped dancing, heedless of the couples swirling around them. "Forced?" he repeated. The narrowing of his eyes was dangerous. "Why, I'll—"

"Anthony, for goodness sake!" Frederica, well aware that people were staring at—and in danger of running into—them, put her hand on his shoulder and would have dragged him into the dance if she could. Although she could not, his response was automatic, and soon they were whirling around the floor again. His jaw remained taut, however, and his eyes glittered. Frederica, swallowing, said, "If it is any consolation to you, Anthony, I no longer find him amusing and will not consider it a loss to avoid his company in the future."

The viscount's eyebrows snapped together. "Is that it, then?" he demanded. "Is the baron the desperate case you referred to? I should have run him through the night he—" The words came to an abrupt end; it was as if he swallowed and almost choked on them.

"The night he . . ." Frederica prompted.

He frowned down at her. "Never mind."

"Well, of all the—" Frederica began.

He stopped her with "Is that it? Has he been opportuning you?"

"No," Frederica said. "The baron just returned to town this day."

"And how do you know that?" Anthony demanded.

"I had spies on the Great North Road watching for him, of course!" she snapped, disliking his tone. When he seemed almost ready to believe her, she shook his shoulder as well as she could for one who had to reach up at such a disadvantage to do so and said, "He said so tonight, Anthony. How else would I know it?"

Chilesworth shrugged the shoulder she had just tried to shake. "The baron has a way with young, naïve women, my dear," he said.

"Well, I am not young and naïve," she began, read the disbelief in his eyes, and glared at him. "And the baron does not have 'a way' with me!"

Chilesworth seemed about to say more but stopped even as she waited. "Well, then," he said, "if not the baron, then what . . ."

"What what?" Frederica demanded when he seemed unable to finish the sentence.

"What did you write me about?"

"Write you?" Her face wore a blank look, and Chilesworth led her out onto a long, shallow balcony as the dance ended. Several other couples had sought its relief from the stuffy ballroom as well and stood talking quietly, out of range of the viscount and his lady. The cool breeze that followed the rain was welcome after the indoor heat of the past few hours, and Frederica raised her head to it, her eyes half-closed.

"What do you mean, Anthony?" She turned to him, her eyes still appreciative of the treat the night had to offer.

He raised an automatic hand to brush back a hair that had escaped its confines and had fallen forward on her brow. "'*Chilesworth*'," he repeated. "'The case is *desperate*. Come at once! Frederica.'"

"Oh!" Frederica's mind moved from her present problems, including Baron Barnsley's recent behavior and the feel of the viscount's hand on her forehead, to those that plagued the rest of her moments. "That!"

"That, Frederica?" the viscount questioned when she turned from him and took a few steps into the shadows. "Are you in some sort of trouble, my dear?"

Frederica seemed to be having trouble finding the words to explain the desperate case to him. "Well, no . . ." she began, her fingers lacing and unlacing in the darkness. "That is, yes . . ."

Chilesworth thought a moment and smiled. "Been dipping deep again, Freddie?"

"Frederica," she corrected, "and I don't know what you mean!"

"I mean, my dear, that if you have gambling debts you are afraid to tell your father about, I will be happy to help you—"

"Of course not!" Frederica's tone was stiff. "I am sure it

is very good of you to say so, Anthony, but I hardly need
your help with money! And if you must know, lately I have
had quite a run of luck at silver loo—" She could feel
the viscount laughing at her in the shadows, and her
backbone grew even stiffer. "I don't know why you laugh,"
she told him.

"Silver loo!" The viscount's shoulders were shaking.
"La, child, what a hardened gamester you are!"

"Oh!" Frederica's chin came up. "Just because I do
not . . . not"—she tried to remember the phrase George
used to describe persons who went far in debt—"run off my
legs . . ." She realized she didn't have it quite right when
he laughed again, and her fury mounted. "And I am not a
child!"

No, the viscount said, she was not, which was another
reason for her to stay away from Baron Barnsley. That
thought effectively stopped his laughter, and he returned to
the question at hand. "Well, what is it, then, Frederica?" he
asked. "What is this desperate case that I must needs come
at once to you for?"

Put like that, it was hard to answer, but she did. "Bride
clothes," Frederica told him.

"What?"

The viscount gaped at her. Perhaps he had caught a fever
in the rain.

"Bride clothes!" Frederica repeated. "Bride clothes! My
mother wishes to buy me bride clothes!"

"Well . . ." The viscount was at a loss. "You hardly
need my help with that, Freddie! Your mother has excellent
taste, and—"

"Of course I don't need your help with bride clothes, you
idiot!"

Chilesworth said he believed he had mentioned to her
before that he did not care to be called an idiot and would
thank her for refraining from doing so. The lady looked as
if she would scream.

"Don't you understand, Anthony? My mother is talking

about bride clothes, and she says that as soon as you are returned to town—and here you are, returned to town!—we must set a date for the wedding, and . . ." Her words trailed off.

Chilesworth, staring at her, heard his stomach rumble again. "Frederica," he said, "I drove through rain today— much rain. It was cold. It was wet. I arrived home hungry, wanting nothing more than my supper and my bed. Instead I found your note, talking of desperate cases. Abandoning my warm fire, I washed, shaved, and dressed—by myself, you understand, my valet is not expected until tomorrow!— and plunged out into the night, to follow you here and find you dancing with that fellow Barnsley and flirting with young Mattington." He ignored her interruptions that she had not wanted to dance with the baron and that she did not *flirt*. "And now you tell me it is all because of *bride clothes*?"

Frederica, watching him with anxious eyes, nodded. She grew highly indignant when her betrothed threw back his head and laughed.

Chapter Nineteen

"WELL, IT IS all very well for you to laugh, Anthony," Frederica said, "for I can see that you do not believe bride clothes concern you—"

Wiping his streaming eyes, the viscount said that no, no, that was true. But as she had so rightly pointed out, while the bride clothes did not concern him, the wedding they portended did.

Frederica agreed. "And that is why the case is desperate!" she told him. "For if we are to set a date, it gives us even less time to . . . to . . ." She seemed to forget to what as he moved forward to take her hand.

"Frederica," he said, "I am hungry."

She gaped up at him. She wasn't sure what she had expected his movement forward to mean, but that wasn't it. "Oh. Well . . ." Her face was doubtful. "There is a buffet laid out upstairs."

"And I am tired."

"Oh?" She did not think it appropriate to tell him to seek one of the Earl of Manfield's beds.

"And I am going home."

"Home?" Surprise and consternation were in her voice. "But, Anthony—"

"Tomorrow," he said, "in the afternoon, I am sure, for I intend to sleep through the morning, I shall call upon you. We will discuss your bride clothes then."

"Anthony," she said, doing her best to convey to him an appropriate sense of urgency, "this is not about bride clothes!"

"Yes, my dear." He kissed her hand, and the warmth of his lips lingered after they were removed. "I know. It is about desperate cases." He put her hand on his forearm and led her back into the ballroom, heedless of her half sentences as she stared up at him. Once inside, they almost collided with Mr. Mattington, who had been trying to appear as inconspicuous as possible as he stood by the long windows.

"Ah, Mattington," the viscount said, beckoning to him. Mr. Mattington's leg trembled but he came forward. "Your dance, wasn't it?"

Chilesworth placed Frederica's hand into that of her young swain and, without looking back, sauntered to the ballroom entrance, exchanging a word or two with acquaintances as he went. At the door he bowed with exquisite grace to his hostess and disappeared.

"Well!" huffed Frederica.

"Yes," replied the happy Mr. Mattington. "Well!" He was beaming and, unable to believe his luck, led Frederica out onto the floor for a country dance.

It was nearly evening when Chilesworth's high-stepping chestnuts pulled up in front of the Forkham mansion the next day, and by then Frederica had fidgeted herself almost to death.

She had refused her mother's invitation to accompany her on several calls to other members of the ton, including the Wrothtons, whom Frederica particularly liked. She also had declined her brother's offer to take a turn around Hyde Park with him, standing resolute even when he offered to let her drive his new team, if she cared to come.

Since Frederica had been pestering him to let her take the horses in hand ever since he had purchased them two weeks earlier, it was a big temptation. Real regret showed in her face as she said, "No, George, I am waiting for Anthony. But"—she brightened—"if you should care to repeat your offer tomorrow . . ."

George said he would see and went out, leaving his sister in expectation of her betrothed's momentary arrival. Expectation had stretched through several hours when he at last came, and by then she was in a rare taking.

Instead of the polite greeting Anthony felt he might have expected, he was met by a frowning Frederica, whose first words were "*Where* have you been?"

Chilesworth raised an eyebrow and held his hands out to the fire that burned in the morning-room grate. "It is very good to see you, too, my dear."

"Don't my-dear me!"

"And in such sunny looks—and sunny temper too!"

Frederica glared at him. "You said you were coming this afternoon."

"And so I have."

"It is nearly evening!"

Chilesworth glanced at the clock on the mantelpiece. "Well," he said, rubbing his hands again, "so it is."

Frederica's eyes narrowed and her tone was dangerous. "Anthony," she said, "do not toy with me."

The viscount looked up at that, and his eyes held a curious half smile. "But of course not, Frederica," he said. "Of course not."

She frowned at him, unable to read that smile. "Well," she demanded. "Are you going to tell me where you've been?"

The viscount opened his eyes wide, in imitation of one of

her own tricks, and in spite of herself Frederica smiled. "Much better," he approved.

"That does not answer my question, my lord," she informed him, voice and face prim.

"No," he agreed, "it does not."

There was silence except for the crackling of the fire until Frederica, unable to bear it, repeated her "Well?"

"Yes, thank you," the viscount said, his voice absent as his eyes returned to the fire. "I am very well."

"Anthony!"

Chilesworth raised a quizzical eyebrow in inquiry, then relented. "I told you last night, Frederica," he said, "that I intended to sleep through today."

She gave the clock her pointed attention. "And you have been in bed all this time?"

The viscount's voice was tranquil as he said he had not. He had risen sometime after noon and had enjoyed the expert attentions of his valet, who had by then arrived. He'd been shaved and tenderly helped into the claret coat he now wore that molded his shoulders to such advantage. Then he'd enjoyed a breakfast on which his chef had outdone himself.

"Remind me to raise that fellow's wages, Frederica," he said, his absent gaze again returning to the fire. "He really is a genius with food."

"I will not!" Frederica cried. "It is no concern of mine if you remember to reward your servants—"

"But if they are to be *our* servants, my dear . . ." The half smile was back, and the eyes that moments ago had been absent were now remarkably keen.

Frederica, taken aback, could only stutter, "But—but—" With a mental shake she pulled herself together and stared up at him. "What do you mean?" she asked.

The viscount's smile broadened. "Well, my dear, if I understood you correctly last night, it is time to set a date for the wedding."

"Yes."

"Our wedding."

"No!"

Chilesworth's mobile eyebrow was used to full advantage. "You have found someone else, then?" he asked, words and tone polite.

"Well, no, but . . ." Frederica hurried to the small writing table that sat in the corner of the room. "I have made a list!" she said.

The viscount looked at her, surprised. "A list?"

Frederica nodded, handing him a piece of paper. "This one is yours," she told him.

The viscount looked down and read, in her fine hand, "Chloe Harthington."

"Chloe Harthington?" he repeated, his shock evident. "Good grief, Frederica, the girl giggles!"

"She is perhaps a little nervous—" Frederica began.

"Incessantly! She never stops!"

Frederica sighed. "How about Arabella?" she asked, referring to the next name on the list. "You *like* Arabella!"

The viscount nodded. "Of course I like Arabella. I have known her forever and have no objection to being related to her by marriage."

Frederica's stomach gave an odd lurch, but she ignored it as she said, "You don't?"

The viscount shook his head. "Not the least objection. She is to marry my cousin Charles next May. He visited me at Chilesworth Manor to tell me. The news is just not about yet."

"Oh!" Frederica's stomach righted itself again. "Well, then . . ." She bit her lip. "How about Miss Scarton? She never giggles, her portion is generous, and she has a most improved mind . . ." The words ran off in light of the viscount's obvious scorn.

"Never giggles?" Chilesworth repeated, looking down at the last name on the the list Frederica had prepared for him.

"How true! Never smiles, either! No, thank you, Freddie—I'd just as soon have you as that Friday-faced chit."

"Well!" Frederica said.

The viscount, realizing he had not been especially complimentary, tried to make it better. "Rather, in fact!" She still did not look appeased. "Frederica?" he tried.

The lady took a turn about the room. "I cannot help feeling that you have not put your heart into looking, Anthony," she complained.

The viscount agreed that might very well be true. Then he asked to see her list.

"My list?" Frederica repeated. She carried it in her hand, and Chilesworth, seated nearby, pointed to it. "Oh. Well. Perhaps the lists weren't such a good idea—" she began, realizing too late what he was about when he reached out and took it from her.

The viscount looked down, then raised his eyes to hers. "So many, Frederica?" he said mockingly. He glanced at the blank paper again.

The lady blushed.

"It seemed like a good idea," she said, attempting to excuse herself.

"Not even your Mr. Mattington is here," he said, crumpling the paper and tossing it into the fire. He meant the words lightly, and was surprised to find her giving them serious consideration.

"Well, the truth is, Anthony, I did consider Mr. Mattington," she said. "He is very biddable, you know, and so good-hearted."

"You don't want biddable, Frederica," Chilesworth said, rising to take her hand. "You'd walk all over the poor fellow."

"Well," she said, turning her head away, "the truth is, I'm rather afraid you're right!" She tried to ignore the viscount's thumb, which was rubbing warm little circles in her palm. "And I should not like myself for that."

"You wouldn't like Mattington for it, either," Chiles-worth assured her.

"No, I suppose not," she conceded. She pulled her hand from his and put it behind her back, taking several steps away before she turned to face him. "Well, Anthony," she said, trying to put on a bright face, "what now?"

"Now?" The viscount's mysterious half smile had been replaced by a full-humored one. "Now, my dear, I suppose you order your bride clothes and we marry!"

Chapter
Twenty

"M-M-*MARRY*?!" Frederica had never heard herself stutter so much in her life, and it annoyed her that she was the one thrown off-kilter while the viscount remained so maddeningly calm. He nodded.

"But you do not wish to marry me!" Frederica said.

Chilesworth's eyes laughed, although his face remained schooled in a polite smile. "Hard to believe, my dear, but I find myself hourly more resigned—even reconciled—to the idea."

"You . . . do?"

He nodded.

Frederica did not believe him. "This is all a hum," she said. "You are saying these things just to provoke me, and then, when I have rung a rare peal over you, you will laugh and tell me you've decided to go off to Brazil, after all." A ray of hope appeared in her eyes. "Is that it, Anthony? Have you decided to visit your uncle?"

The viscount assured her he had not.

"But, *why*?" She almost wailed the word, and Chilesworth smiled.

"Why won't I go to Brazil?" he said. "I believe, my dear, that we have been all over that."

"No," she said. "No. Why are you suddenly so ready to marry?"

Chilesworth hastened to assure her that he was not really *ready* to marry; but if it was to be, it had occurred to him that he would just as soon be married to her as to anyone. In fact, he was growing, as he'd said earlier, almost resigned to the idea.

He paused, then asked, "And you, Freddie?"

"Frederica," she mumbled, her chin tucked almost to her chest so he could not see her face. He let go of one hand and used his free hand to raise her head.

"Frederica," he said, "how do you feel about . . . me?"

"Well . . ." The lady looked into the fire. "I suppose—when you are not lecturing, or prosing at me, or coming high-handed over my wishes—that you can be almost . . . pleasant."

The words seemed to surprise her as much as they amused him. "Pleasant, Freddie?" he repeated. "My dear, what high praise!"

"And provoking," she added, her eyes returning to his face. "Deliberately provoking."

He grinned and released her chin. "I am promised to my cousin tonight, Frederica, and tomorrow we leave for his estate for several days. While I am gone, think about our conversation. I know it's a shock—we tried for so long to think of ways to avoid this marriage that it is rather difficult to think of it as something to agree to. I was surprised myself when I found . . ." He did not complete the sentence, merely raising her hand to his lips and brushing them gently over her knuckles in a way that made her breath tighten.

When he released her, she stared up at him, searching for the commonplace. "You are going out of town again, Anthony?" she tried. "But you just got back!"

He grinned at her. "Will you miss me, Frederica?"

She refused to say, biting her lip in vexation. "What am I going to tell my parents?" she asked. "They are going to ask what date we've set, and here you are, trotting out of town again and leaving me to deal with everything." The injustice of it all struck her, and she glared at him. "This is just like you, Anthony!"

"Yes, my dear, it is. And when I return, I fully expect to find another note urging me to your rescue and speaking of desperate cases!"

"Urging you to my . . ." Frederica's eyes widened. "Did you really think I was in trouble, Anthony?" He did not respond, and she thought further. "Then that is why you arrived so late, and Higgins said you had been here." She touched his arm. "Why, Anthony!" she said. "That was very good of you!"

"More chivalrous than you can believe, in fact!" The words were light, and he gave her cheek a careless tap before heading for the door. "I know. I could hardly believe it of myself!"

She stopped him with, "But, Anthony—when will you return? Our engagement ball is the end of next week, and—"

He turned, one hand on the door latch, "Do not fear, my dear. I shall return in plenty of time. I expect to be back Wednesday next."

"But that is just two days before the ball!"

"Plenty of time," the viscount assured her. "Plenty of time."

The frown on Frederica's face as he left the room made it apparent she did not think so.

Frederica found herself much distracted from her daily rounds in the next few days—so much so that the countess, after several days of watching her daughter pick at her food and answer quite at random to any questions put to her, was moved to ask if Frederica was feeling quite the thing.

Frederica, looking up at the breakfast table to find the eyes of her parents and her brother fixed upon her, put down her fork and said, "Was there something . . . ?" looking from one to the other of them.

The countess, realizing her question had not been heard, asked again. "Are you feeling all right, Frederica?" She reached out to touch her daughter's wrist. "If not, we could ask Dr. Thorkle to call."

Frederica appeared so surprised by the question that her mother was at least convinced that whatever ailed her daughter was not physical. "Dr. Thorkle?" Frederica repeated. "Whatever for?"

"Well, my dear"—the countess spread her hands in a helpless gesture—"you seem so . . . listless."

"Moped to death," George corrected. Both the countess and Frederica frowned at him.

"No, Mama," Frederica said. "I am not ill. Just . . . thinking."

"Oh." The earl and countess exchanged glances, with each other and then with their son.

"Thinking," George repeated.

Frederica, who had picked up her fork and once again was running it through her eggs without stopping to pick up a bite, nodded. Her brother rolled his eyes. "Then think about driving out with me this morning," he invited. "I'm going to exercise my new grays."

"That's nice, George," Frederica said, without answering his invitation. George raised an eyebrow in his mother's direction, and the countess nodded.

"Come along, Freddie," George urged. "I'll let you drive, if you like."

He knew something was wrong when she did not correct his use of her childhood name, and he grew seriously alarmed when she said that it wasn't necessary that she drive, if he would rather do so.

"Of course you can drive," George said, tossing down

his napkin and walking around to her side of the table to hold back her chair for her. "Can't think of very many people I'd think my horses safer with!"

Frederica rose as he put his arm under her elbow, and offered him a dreamy smile. "Really, George?" she said. "That's nice."

George, who had considered it the highest of praise—and certainly praise he had heretofore never bestowed upon her—was stunned.

They had driven several miles in silence, Frederica answering in monosyllables her brother's attempts at conversation, when George pulled his team to the side of the road and said, "All right, Freddie. Spill it."

"Spill what, George?" she asked. Growing aware that they'd stopped, she looked around. "Was there something you wanted me to see?"

Frankly, her brother said, he'd like her to see what a cake she was making of herself! If he'd thought to jolt her with that, it did not work. Frederica looked surprised but did not take umbrage. George grew more worried.

"Is it your engagement, Freddie?" he asked, putting to her directly the one question he had not wanted to get into. "Is it Anthony?"

Frederica sighed and looked away. "Yes, George," she said, the words low. "It is Anthony."

George sighed. "I am sure Mama and Papa meant well—" he began, but got no further.

Frederica turned to him. "Anthony says he is resigned to marrying me, George!"

"He—what?" There must have been some movement in his hands, for the team started forward. George pulled on the reins, and the horses, after a head toss in his direction, stopped.

"He is resigned—even reconciled—to marrying me! And—oh, George—I do not wish him to be!"

To her brother's horror two large tears eased out of Frederica's eyes and down her cheeks. "Here now, Freddie," he said. "I say . . ."

He reached into his pocket for a handkerchief and handed it to her. "The thing is, Freddie," he said, watching in great helplessness as she applied it to her eyes, "I thought—I think we all thought—that is, you seemed to be getting along so much better with Anthony the last few weeks."

"The last few weeks he has been out of town," Frederica wailed. "Is it any wonder we get along when he is not around, George?"

"Well, before that," her brother said, giving her shoulder an awkward pat. "You seemed to be getting along well before that."

Frederica nodded. "I know." She gulped. "I didn't know it then, of course, but I have given it a great deal of thought these past few days, and I find that now—now—now I know it. And Anthony is *resigned* to marrying me!"

It took George some time to discover that the crux of Frederica's problem was not the idea of marrying Anthony but the viscount's resignation to the plan.

"I do not want him to be . . . *resigned*, George! I do not want to marry a man who is . . . *resigned*!"

Her brother bit his lip to keep from laughing. "But, Freddie," he said, trying to ignore the damage she was doing to his linen handkerchief, "are you saying that you want to marry Anthony?"

His sister sat bolt upright and glared at him. "I am saying no such thing, George!" she told him. "And I will thank you not to be spreading such rumors." She thought, and her glare grew. "*Especially* not to Anthony!"

"But, Freddie—" George began.

"Frederica," she corrected. "And if you brought me out here for a drive, George, I wish you would drive!"

Obediently her brother gave his team the office to start, and after they had bowled along for several minutes he handed her the reins. She took them in her competent hands and gave her full attention to driving, which was good, for it allowed her brother to watch her. It was clear to him that she labored under the delusion that Viscount Chilesworth could be brought to do something because he was told to do so, and not, in the end, because he wanted to do it. George, who had no such doubts on that question, gave a soundless whistle. It was almost as clear to him that his sister would not believe his insight, but still, he supposed he ought to try.

"You know, Freddie," he told her, looking out at the passing landscape, "Anthony is a very hard man to drive."

"I know that, George." Frederica's words were absent as she watched the horses. "He will never let me take the reins, no matter what."

No, George said, that wasn't what he meant. What he meant was, if Anthony really didn't want to marry her, he wouldn't, no matter what the threat over his head.

"Brazil, George?" His sister's eyebrow quirked, and it was apparent she considered that enough of a threat for anyone.

It was a powerful threat, George allowed; but Anthony wasn't likely, in the end, to let it weigh with him if he really had his face set against marriage.

"But, George." Frederica sighed. "I don't just want to know that his face is no longer set against it. I want to know that he is set *toward* it—and with—with—"

She did not say *with me*, but George understood. Or thought he did.

"Perhaps," he told her, putting his hand on her wrist, "you should ask him."

Frederica sighed again. Sometimes George could be as dense as other men. Why should she ask Anthony, when the viscount had already told her he was . . . resigned?

Chapter
Twenty-One

"AH, LADY FREDERICA."

Frederica, looking up from her place in the Schevington music room, frowned. She knew the voice without seeing the speaker, and it was not one she wished to hear.

"Baron Barnsley," she acknowledged, looking away. Her eyes sought George, who had accompanied her to the Schevingtons' that evening under the guise of escort but who had abandoned her the moment he found the daughter of the house, Cassandra Schevington. The baron, interpreting her gaze, smiled.

"It seems you are left quite unprotected, my dear," he told her. "Your escorts have a way of disappearing, don't they?"

That drew Frederica's eyes back to him, and they flashed fire. Her voice, however, was schooled to sweetness as she answered, "I was not aware that I am in need of protection, Baron Barnsley. And I am sure I do not know what you mean about disappearing escorts."

The baron laughed and took the seat next to her, to her private dismay. "You have courage, Lady Frederica," he said. "Courage and intelligence. I have always liked that about you."

Frederica pointedly gazed away.

"And what I mean about your escorts is, your betrothed seems to be leaving town a great deal these days, and now your brother has abandoned you in favor of Miss Schevington."

Frederica returned her gaze to his. "I do not see that Anthony's comings and goings are any business of mine—I mean, yours!" she said.

The baron's chuckle was soft, and his eyes appeared to see a great deal more than Frederica wished him to. "I believe you were right the first time, weren't you, my dear?"

"What?"

The chuckle was softer still, deep in his throat. Frederica, who did not like the way he laughed at her, or the manner in which his eyes mocked her, felt her cheeks growing hot.

"Come now, my lady," the baron said, watching her. He sat, seemingly relaxed, leaning back in the chair, but Frederica saw the fingers of his left hand tense and flex. She frowned at the action even as he continued. "How long do you and Chilesworth intend to keep up this masquerade?"

Frederica's eyes widened in spite of herself. The baron chuckled again. "M-m-masquerade?" she queried, striving for her earlier tone of polite boredom. It was clear the baron was not fooled.

"But of course, my lady," he said, his eyes traveling from her face to a place lower before returning again. Frederica's color heightened. "You don't really expect me to believe that you and the oh so good viscount are really in love?"

"I—I—". Frederica was saved from replying by a touch on her shoulder.

"Ah, there you are, my dear," said another voice she knew, and her heart sank. A moment earlier she had thought she would welcome any diversion, but now . . . She looked up into the enigmatic face of the Earl of Manning-ham.

"My lord!" she said. Her hand touched his forearm in a way that made him study her eyes more closely, and he must have read something she wasn't aware was there, because his hand came up to cover hers, even as he bowed to the baron.

"Baron Barnsley," the earl said. Frederica marveled at how a master of the social graces could make the pronunciation of a man's name, uttered in a politely cold tone, an insult.

Not by look or deed did the baron betray he was anything but delighted to see Frederica's future father-in-law. "My lord," he said, rising, "it has been some time since we last met."

Manningham looked down his nose at the other man. "Has it?" he replied before turning his back in a dismissal the baron could not fail to understand. Frederica saw Barnsley flush for a moment before regaining his carefully schooled expression of cynical boredom. With an elaborate bow to her the baron smiled and sauntered away.

"My lord, I—" Frederica began, but was stopped when Manningham put a finger to her lips.

"My dear," he said, "I would like a word with you, if you would not mind." He glanced around to where others in the room were resuming their seats for the next musical number, and then toward the front of the room.

"Oh, no." He sighed, his eyes reminding Frederica of Anthony's when he told a whisker in just that tone. "Mrs. Schevington is about to play her viola and we must miss it. I am devastated, my dear. And you?"

Already he was walking her to the door, and Frederica, who knew that he, like she, was more relieved than both could say, bit her lip. "Devastated," she managed. The earl smiled.

Once through the music room door he led her down the

hall, saying as they went, "I am sure my friend Schevington will not mind if we use his library for a moment." He pushed open the door and ushered Frederica through it. Both halted at the sight of other occupants silhouetted by the soft glow of the fire burning low in the grate.

"Oh!" said Cassandra Schevington, whipping behind her back the hand that George had held a moment earlier. "Oh!"

George coughed. "Um," he said, trying to ignore the light in his sister's eyes, "um . . . were you . . . looking for me, Frederica?"

"Yes," the earl answered, before Frederica could even begin to tease her brother. "Yes, we were, George. We thought you and Miss Schevington would want to know"—and here he smiled at Cassandra— "that your mama is just beginning her viola solo in the music room."

"Oh!" said Cassandra. "Oh!"

"Yes," George replied, seconding her. "Oh. Well, we wouldn't want to miss that."

He made a polite motion for the lady to precede him, and she did, pausing as she came even with the earl and Frederica to say, "You won't—that is—"

"This way, Cassandra," George said, taking her hand and placing it on his forearm, his own hand remaining on hers for comfort. "We would not want to miss your mama's solo." Frederica could tell from his expression that there was little he would like more than missing said solo, and she hid her laugh behind an unconvincing cough that made her brother frown at her.

"No," Miss Schevington agreed, ducking her head under the earl's amused stare. "Oh! No, of course not!"

The room seemed very quiet after George and Cassandra departed; even the fire contented itself with only an occasional muted snap. Manningham escorted Frederica to a tall-backed leather chair by the fire, then leaned an elbow on the mantelpiece, looking down at the grate.

"My lord, I—" Frederica began.

The earl looked up and smiled. "I do not believe I have told you, Frederica," he said, "how happy I am that you are to be part of our family."

Frederica gulped. "Baron Barnsley—" she tried.

The earl gazed into the fire again. "Frederica," he interrupted, cutting off her next words even before she could decide what to say, "I wish to tell you a story."

"A . . . a story?" she repeated. He smiled at her surprise.

"It is a story I am not supposed to know," he said. Each word came slowly, as if he still might call them back. "I never repeated it before, because there has been no reason to do so. Still, I think you should know, and neither Anthony nor George will tell you, I am certain, because they feel honor bound not to." He glanced her way and paused.

"If you would rather not, my lord," Frederica began, surprising herself. She wished to know, and yet she did not; if it was a matter of honor . . .

The earl shook his head. "I believe, my dear, that you have met my niece, Eliza?"

Frederica nodded. Eliza! So that was the lady!

The earl, watching her, frowned slightly. "Was there something, Frederica?"

She shook her head, lowering her eyes and waiting.

"When Eliza came out," the earl said, and his voice carried the note of faraway memory, "perhaps nine years ago now, she took the town by storm. She was a beautiful girl—*is* a beautiful woman—and an heiress, besides. All of London was at her feet. We were so proud of her, my wife and I, for we think of Eliza as a daughter. Her father, my brother, died so early, and her mother soon afterward. She lived with us a great deal during her growing up, and Anthony has always thought of her as a sister."

He stopped a moment and contemplated the fire. His head turned toward Frederica, who was watching him. "You have met Eliza, haven't you, Frederica?"

She nodded. "When I was twelve. You visited one summer."

The earl nodded. "I remember." His concentration returned to the fire, and Frederica waited.

"One of Eliza's suitors," the earl said, "was Baron Barnsley. He was most insistent. Even then the baron was in need of a rich wife—and he can be most engaging with the ladies. My own wife used, in the past, to say she found him quite amusing. I don't see it, myself, but . . ."

Frederica was glad the darkness hid her blush. She had told Anthony the same thing about the baron, and he had not seen it, either.

"It was almost the end of the season," the earl continued, as if from far away. "My wife and I were called out of town to care for an ill aunt of hers. We left Eliza with a cousin of my wife's. Eliza had informed us, not two days earlier, that she had decided to marry Reginald Plumton, a nice young man with a small estate in Yorkshire. We were surprised by Eliza's announcement. We liked Mr. Plumton well enough, but we knew that Eliza could have looked much higher for a mate. Still, we had promised her that the choice was hers, and we believed she would choose well." He stopped a moment and reflected.

"Obviously she did, too. She and Reginald are very happy." He sighed. "Eliza was never really one for town life. Perhaps it was because her own parents died so early that she is so happy being part of and caring for her own family now. I don't know. Still . . ." He gave himself a shake, as if he had just recalled where he was and whom he was talking to. He smiled at Frederica. "Am I boring you, my dear?" he asked.

"Oh, no, my lord!" Frederica assured him. "I am thinking as you speak of how much I would like to renew my acquaintance with Mrs. Plumton!"

The earl nodded. "You would like her, Frederica, I am sure."

Frederica agreed and waited.

The earl continued. "While we were from town, my wife and I," he said, "Baron Barnsley invited Eliza to go driving with him. A kindhearted girl, she felt she should be the one to tell him of her marriage plans, so he would not hear the news elsewhere. She acquiesced to his invitation. Little did she know that the baron had already heard gossip of her engagement and had decided to carry her off to Gretna Green. She was taken in his phaeton to his carriage, on the outskirts of town, and they started north—"

"Kidnapped!" Frederica said. Her eyes flashed fire. "Of all the perfidious—"

The earl smiled. It was a smile that made Frederica's blood run cold. "Quite," Manningham said. "But quite ingenious, too—at least, so the baron thought. With me out of town he believed Eliza had no one to protect her or to follow them. I suppose that it never occurred to him that someone he considered a mere boy, down from school on holiday, would start out."

"Anthony!" Frederica breathed.

The earl smiled again. "Anthony," he agreed. "And your brother, George."

"George?"

The earl nodded. "My source says George would not let Anthony go without him; in fact, they almost came to blows over it."

Frederica's look was one of disgust. "They would," she agreed. "And meanwhile the baron was getting farther and farther away."

The earl almost laughed. "You understand my son and your brother very well, Frederica," he said approvingly.

She shrugged a shoulder in disgust. "They often act in that manner," she said.

This time he did laugh. "Yes, well . . ." he said. "They also succeeded. They caught up with the carriage that night, and there, on the road, Anthony challenged the baron to a duel."

"A duel!" Even though she had evidence her betrothed had survived, Frederica felt her heart tighten.

The earl nodded. "The baron is known for his skill as a duelist, Frederica," he told her. "And my son was barely eighteen."

"Oh!" Frederica put a hand over her eyes. The earl returned his gaze to the fire.

"I am told, although I did not see it, that the fighting was furious. It was obvious the baron had the greater skill, but just when it appeared Anthony might be in real danger, they came within distance of the carriage where Eliza sat. Both of the men were intent on their footwork and swordplay and little else, and Eliza—bless her soul!—saw the baron's back to her and swung the door open with all her might, catching him as he threw his head back to avoid one of Anthony's plunges. She knocked him out cold."

"Good for Eliza!" Frederica cheered.

The earl laughed. "Yes," he agreed. "Good for Eliza! Anthony, of course, was furious, because he wanted to run the baron through, and there was George, telling him it was bad form to skewer an unconscious man—"

Frederica's head moved up and down and she rolled her eyes. "I can just hear them," she said. "And I imagine Anthony wanted to wait around until the baron woke up so they could fight again and he could probably get himself killed—"

"He did," the earl agreed.

"Men!" Frederica said.

"Yes." Frederica had the feeling the earl was laughing at her now, although he stood in the shadows and she could not see his face. "I understand that is what Eliza said. And that she gave Anthony and George a rare tongue-lashing and told them that if they'd come to rescue her, then they should rescue her, for heaven's sakes, and not leave it all up to her to do!" Frederica giggled.

"Oh," she said. "I wish I could have seen that!"

The earl smiled. "I rather wish I could have seen it too. Although"—and here the laughter vanished from his voice—"had I been there, I would not have been as gallant toward the baron as Anthony."

Frederica felt a shiver run down her back and realized she was clutching her hands together so tightly that her fingers hurt. Releasing them, she took a deep breath.

"I am glad you have told me this story, my lord," she said.

The earl came forward to offer his arm. It was apparent their tete-à-tête was ended. "My dear," Manningham said, with one of his graceful bows that put the rest of the gentlemen of the ton to shame, "I thought you should know."

Chapter
Twenty-Two

MANNINGHAM AND FREDERICA returned to the musicale just in time to add their applause to that of the others in the room. From the faces of many it was apparent they were applauding the end of the performance more than the performance itself, and the earl grinned. Frederica, seeing what Anthony would look like in perhaps thirty years, caught her breath. She almost hoped that Anthony wouldn't grow so perspicacious, at least not in regard to his wife; although such perspicacity could be very helpful where the viscount's children were concerned.

She blushed to find herself thinking about Anthony's wife and children, and gave herself a mental shake just as Manningham whispered in her ear, "It appears Mrs. Schevington has given another one of her sterling performances."

"That everyone would pay twelve pounds sterling to avoid," Frederica whispered back. It was a jest she had heard her brother and Chilesworth make many times before.

"No need to wonder where you heard that," the earl said, satisfied. Frederica was embarrassed that she blushed and lowered her eyes.

"You know, Frederica, I realize that when you and Anthony first announced your engagement, neither of you was very pleased with the pact." His lips lifted as her expressive eyes rose to his at his pause. "Even if you did then decide that you had been attracted to each other all along and each of your quarrels was a 'lover's spat.'"

Frederica, remembering the night of her engagement and the conversations she and Anthony had had with their fathers at Almack's, turned even redder.

"But now," the earl said, and his eyes were kind, "I hope you are perhaps more . . . reconciled to the match?" There was a clear question in his face, and Frederica sighed.

"Anthony is, my lord," she said, looking off toward the corner where George stood, saying his farewells to Cassandra. "Anthony is . . . resigned." She could not stop the second sigh that followed her first.

"And you, Frederica?"

She did not meet his inquiring gaze. "I, my lord," she said, still looking away, "do not wish to be . . . resigned."

"Ah." The wealth of meaning behind that sound was not lost on Frederica, who risked a hasty glance in the earl's direction before looking away again. She had seen amusement in his face and wondered at it. "Then perhaps it is a love match, after all," Manningham said.

Her eyes rose to his face in painful confusion. "I . . . I . . ." she began.

"My son," Manningham said, his words as calm as his expression, "is a sap-skull. You must try not to hold that against him, my dear. He has never done this before, you know."

Unsure of his meaning, Frederica could not help but frown at his words, and at the face that seemed to understand more than she cared to have him understand.

"Chilesworth, my lord," Frederica said, "says you have a way of knowing everything."

This time she *knew* there was amusement in the earl's

face. "It has been helpful to me, Frederica, to have him think so."

"But—" She was prevented from continuing the conversation by George's arrival to take her home. On the short drive to the Forkham mansion she could not decide if her brother's appearance had been a relief—for it had got her away from those knowing eyes—or a bother.

Viscount Chilesworth arrived back in London not one but two days before he was expected. His first stop after his arrival home, to change his clothes and enjoy some of his chef's excellent work, was at his betrothed's. Frederica was not home, he found, but George was. They spoke.

Chilesworth, after leaving the Forkham mansion, made his next stop Manningham House, where he was pleased, he told the butler who had known him since he was a child, to find his father at home. Saying he would just surprise the earl, he went down the hall and entered the library unannounced. Manningham, seated before several letters at his desk, looked up with a slight furrow to his brow, but it cleared at the sight of his son.

"Anthony," the earl said, nodding.

"Father," the viscount replied.

Their transports completed, the earl motioned his son to the chair across from him, saying as he did so, "That is a tolerable port on the sideboard, Anthony. You may help yourself and pour a glass for me, if you please."

Chilesworth moved obediently to the table and poured himself and his father glasses of the wine. He crossed to the earl's desk and handed Manningham a filled goblet before settling himself in the proscribed chair.

"You are back early, I believe," the earl said, when his son seemed in no hurry to speak.

The viscount shrugged. "Charles and I were able to complete our business early, and we both found we had no real taste for the country right now."

Manningham smiled. "Of course," he said. At his son's inquiring glance his smile grew. "There being much stronger attractions in the city right now."

The earl was pleased to see his son look embarrassed.

"Yes, well," Anthony began, then stopped. "I have just come from Forkham mansion," he said.

"I am not surprised."

"Frederica was from home—out shopping with her mother."

"And after your early return, too!" The amusement in his father's eyes made the viscount's color deepen.

"George was home, though." Chilesworth took a gulp of his wine.

"Was he, now?" The earl was watching his son with interest, running one finger around the rim of his goblet as he waited.

"George says that you and Frederica had a private tête-à-tête at the Schevington musicale the other night, Father." At the earl's calm nod, one of the viscount's mobile eyebrows rose. There was a hint of humor in his eyes as he asked, "What were you about, my lord? I'd hate to think my own father was trying to cut me out."

Manningham smiled, a smile Anthony knew well, and said, "Do you think I could, Anthony? Then perhaps it is an even better thing than I have long thought that I do so much love my wife."

"Now *see* here—" the viscount began, stopping when he saw his father's smile grow even more silky. "That is—" Chilesworth gulped his wine again and gave his sire a suspicious stare. "I take it, Father, that you do not care to tell me the topic of your conversation?"

The earl ignored the question as he posed one of his own. "And did your friend George tell you, too, that Baron Barnsley also was at the Schevington musicale?" His polite sip of his wine was in direct contrast to his son's noisy gulp.

"Barnsley?" It was apparent from the surprise on the

viscount's face that George had neglected to include that piece of information. "Well, no . . ."

Manningham smiled. "I would not be at all surprised," he said, "if George did not even notice." At Anthony's puzzled expression he added, "Cassandra Schevington was quite in looks that evening."

"Oh." Chilesworth understood and nodded. His father nodded back.

"I'm surprised Barnsley was invited to the Schevington's—" Chilesworth began, thinking aloud.

"I am sure he was not." The earl sipped his wine. "But his cousin, Mrs. Luxton, was, and if he came as her escort, what could Schevington do? Short of barring him from the house—a tad melodramatic, we are, I am sure, agreed—there was nothing for Schevington to do but let the man in and watch his daughter closely, which he did, I'm sure; and put cotton in his ears when his wife started to play, and which I also am sure he did, although I did not witness it."

Chilesworth laughed. "Isn't it odd that someone as pleasant as Louisa Luxton should have a cousin as abominable as Barnsley?"

"Oh, I don't know." The earl gave the question his careful consideration. "I have often noticed that family members can be very dissimiliar in matters of finesse."

The viscount was not sure what his father meant by that, but believing it might be something to his detriment, he decided not to ask. Instead he said, "But that still does not explain, sir, why you felt it necessary to engage Frederica in private conversation."

The earl's gaze was bland as he met his son's. "Do I now need your permission to speak to someone, Anthony?"

"Why, no, of course not, Father! It is just that—that—"

Satisfied by his son's startled expression and hasty words that he had quite effectively just reduced Chilesworth to the age of twelve, Manningham continued. "But if you must know, I was rescuing beauty in distress."

"What?"

It was apparent Chilesworth was not following, and the earl sighed. For a moment he wondered if he had been just such a trial to his own father; several of their conversations when he was Anthony's age flashed through his mind. Perhaps, the earl thought, his own father had suffered more.

"I saw Barnsley talking to Frederica," the earl said. "She did not seem to be enjoying the conversation. I took her away from it."

The viscount's brow darkened at the words, and Chilesworth set his glass down with a snap. "And where was George through all this? If he is going to serve as his sister's escort, I would expect him to—"

The vision of his son as the last word on propriety and suitable expectations was so novel to the earl that he blinked. "But I told you, Anthony," Manningham said. "Cassandra Schevington was in such looks that night!"

"Oh." Chilesworth was disgusted. "I suppose, sir," he said, after several moments of cogitation, "that I am in your debt."

"Oh, more than you know, Anthony," the earl assured him, the ghost of a smile lingering in his eyes and making his son suspicious. "More than you know."

Chilesworth frowned at his father for several moments before saying, "And I suppose you are not going to tell me what you and Frederica talked about after you took her away from Barnsley?"

A tranquil earl assured him he was not.

The viscount chewed on his lip, a nervous habit he had developed in early childhood and one that always betrayed deep thought. The earl smiled.

"Well, then," the viscount said, rising. "I'll just be going."

The earl nodded. "It is always a pleasure to have you honor me with your company, Anthony," he said. His son heard the gentle irony behind the words and looked uncomfortable. The last conversation he had had with his father in this room had concerned Frederica Farthingham too. And the conversation before that . . .

He could not remember it, but he had the awful feeling his father did.

The earl returned his attention to his letters, and the viscount was almost at the door when Manningham looked up and said, "Anthony?"

Chilesworth turned.

"Have you told your betrothed that you love her, Anthony?"

"Have I—" The viscount gaped at his father. "Have I—"

"You do love her, of course." The words contained such certainty that Chilesworth only continued to stare. At his son's look of astonishment the earl chided him. "Come, come, Anthony! Surely you have realized that by now!"

The viscount gulped and swallowed. "I do not see, Father—" he began.

The earl ignored him. "When you love the person you are betrothed to, it is considered polite to tell them so," the earl continued, in the same tone used to instruct his son in the social graces years ago. "It is customary, Anthony."

"Yes, well," Chilesworth said, "I suppose it is, if you know that the person you are betrothed to also—" He stopped, and it was apparent he was going no further. "Trying to conduct my courtship for me now, are you, Father?" he asked.

Manningham shrugged. "I have it on the best of authority, Anthony, that you are now . . . resigned to your marriage." It was the biggest hint the earl felt he could give his son without betraying a lady's confidence, but the viscount did not take it.

"And you would like to gloat over that," Chilesworth said, his smile tinged with the faintest touch of bitterness. "Having proved that once again, you are right. Well, Father . . ." The viscount opened the door and walked through it, turning back just long enough to add, "Let us hope that Forkham was right where his child is concerned, too!"

The earl waited until he was sure his son was well away from the door before he started to laugh.

Chapter
Twenty-Three

FREDERICA WAS SURPRISED, upon her return to Forkham mansion, to hear that Anthony was back in London. She was even more surprised to hear he had left a message that he would be by that evening to escort her to the Humphreys' masquerade ball.

Now, as they stood on the steps leading to the Humphrey ballroom, she in her violet domino and he in black, their faces half-concealed by the masks that were de rigueur at these events, she told him of her surprise and was stunned when he replied, "Yes, well, if your family will not look after you when I am not about—"

"What?" Frederica, thinking of all the times she had wished her father, mother, and brother would be a little less diligent where she was concerned, could think of nothing else to say.

Chilesworth lowered his voice so those around them would not hear. "George told me you were closeted in the Schevington library with my father recently."

"He did?" Here was a prime example of those times Frederica wished her brother would show a little less concern.

The viscount nodded. "And my father told me why."

"He *did*?"

"Barnsley," Chilesworth replied, before realizing that his last statement had raised more than the to-be-expected surprise.

His suspicions increased when Frederica, relieved, replied. "Oh, yes. Barnsley." She waved the ostrich-feather fan, died lavender to complement her costume, back and forth several times to cool her suddenly hot cheeks. "You need no longer be concerned about Barnsley, Anthony."

"I needn't?" Now it was the viscount's turn to sound surprised.

Frederica's head moved from side to side in rhythm with the movement of the fan. "I no longer find him amusing," she said.

"But my father said Barnsley was bothering you."

It occurred to Frederica that Anthony's father could be a little less concerned with her business also—or at least with what he shared of it with his son. "You needn't worry about Barnsley, Anthony," she told him as they moved up a step. They would be next to greet their host and hostess. "I can take care of myself."

The words, carelessly uttered, would prove prophetic before the night was over.

Frederica returned to the ballroom and gazed in consternation at the flood of people bowing and skipping there. Her last partner had stepped on her gown, causing it to rip, and she had retired to pin it up with the expert help of Lady Humphrey's maid. Anthony had said he would wait for her by the potted palm, but there were at least twelve potted palms in the ballroom, and by eight of them stood a tall man swathed in black. She had just decided which must be the viscount and was starting in that direction when a footman approached and, with a bow, said, "Begging your pardon, my lady, but the gentleman in black said he would await you at the end of the small walk in the garden, by the cupola."

Relieved that she had not approached the wrong gentleman, Frederica cast one glance in the direction she had almost gone before nodding and starting off the opposite way. The unidentified man certainly *looked* like Anthony—and how she would twit the viscount about it! Waiting by the potted palm indeed! And now what was this, an illicit meeting in the Humphreys' garden? It seemed an odd choice for a man who suddenly had become Mr. Propriety—although, she thought with a frown, he had always been that way where she was concerned. She would twit him about that, too, although as she walked along she surmised that he had chosen the cupola as the one spot they might have a few moments alone together, to talk over the date they would select with their parents for their wedding—or to discuss how they were to tell their families the wedding was not to take place. Odd that the latter thought no longer made her as happy as it once had.

Lost in her thoughts, Frederica was almost at the cupola when she caught the sound of someone behind her. She half turned, just in time to throw up a protesting hand as something soft and black and tangling enveloped her.

"Be easy, Lady Frederica," she heard a voice say as she struggled to pull from her the cape that covered her head and shoulders and fell to below her knees. "I mean you no harm."

For one moment, recognizing that voice, Frederica stopped fighting, stunned. It was a moment her assailant took advantage of, and when next she moved, it was to find that her arms were held tight to her sides by what she could only surmise was a rope, and she was being half dragged, half carried away.

"Barnsley!" she screamed at the top of her voice. "Barnsley, you—"

The baron stopped, and Frederica half choked as his hand

came up to cover her mouth, pushing some of the cape's cloth into it. "Hush now, my dear," he said in that soft voice of his that she now hated. "I can't have you screaming the house down, can I? Think how embarrassing!"

"Mmmph!" said Frederica, kicking out with all her might. "Mmmmph!"

She heard the baron's intake of breath and knew her feet had done their work. She kicked again, but without success, as Barnsley hauled her up onto his shoulder and clenched one strong arm behind her knees. In a few minutes she was dropped facedown onto something soft, and before she could right herself, she was aware of motion, the crack of a whip, and the clop of hooves on stone.

A carriage, she thought. *I am in a carriage and we are heading . . .* She could not see and she could not know, but somehow she was sure they were heading north. North. Beside her, the baron said, "Only a little while longer, Frederica, and then I will release you." He had righted her on the seat, and for a moment his hand rested on her knee. She kicked out at him and he chuckled.

"As I said once before, my dear, you have courage. I like that in a woman. But"—there was something in the word that warned her, even as she prepared to kick at him again—"should you continue in this unladylike manner, I shall be forced to tie your feet together. I believe we both would regret that, now wouldn't we?"

Frederica had her doubts as to whether the baron would regret anything that might help him gain his ends, but she knew that she would regret such an action very much, and she subsided.

"Very wise," drawled her companion. The carriage seat creaked, and she could picture him settling back more comfortably to watch the edge of the city flash by. Frederica, to occupy her mind, spent the time—the next forty minutes? two hours? It was hard to tell with her face covered and her hands tied—entertaining herself with mind pictures of appropriate punishments for the baron. These ranged from boiling in oil to banishment from her kingdom, and all of them cheered her greatly.

She had no idea how far they had gone when she felt the carriage slow, then stop. She was picked up and carried a short distance before being put down on what felt like a solid floor. Moments later the bonds holding her arms fell away, and she snatched the cape from her head to glare at the baron.

"Frederica—" he began, starting to take her arm.

"*Don't* touch me!" she said. "Don't you *dare* touch me."

A smile of amusement touched his lips; he made her a polite bow and stood aside, pointing toward a chair. "Pray be seated, my lady."

Frederica, nose in the air, swept toward the chair, her domino held tightly around her. From what she could surmise, they were in the private room of a small inn. It was old, she could tell, and although clean enough, it showed signs of disrepair. An indifferent fire burned in the fireplace and did little to warm the room. The tallow candles on the table smoked, and Frederica sneezed in spite of herself.

"God bless you," said the baron.

Frederica directed his way a glance that would freeze water and said nothing.

Again the baron smiled. "You are perhaps surprised by my actions tonight," he began.

Frederica inclined her head as if they were in her mother's drawing room. "Not at all," she said, her tone polite. "I am told you are in the habit of doing this."

The baron's smile almost disappeared. "So." He more expelled than said the word, and his voice was rueful. "I did not think Anthony would tell you about Eliza."

"Anthony did not."

"Oh." He thought he understood. "Your brother, then—"

"My brother," Frederica said with heavy rebuke, "does not carry tales."

The baron stood, one eyebrow raised, as he waited for her to tell him where she had heard the story. When she did not, he shrugged and said, "I don't suppose it matters where you heard it."

Frederica inclined her head in agreement.

The baron gave his most attractive smile. "The thing is, Lady Frederica, I find myself in something of a bind."

"Funny." The word was very, very dry, and Frederica directed her eyes to the rope that had been used to tie her arms. "I found myself in a bind only recently."

His laughter was genuine. "I believe," he told her, "that we shall deal together very well."

"I believe," Frederica told him, "that we shall not deal together at all."

The baron shook his head. "I am distressed to disagree with you, Lady Frederica, but I must. You see, I am in need of a wife—"

"A *rich* wife?" Frederica said with scorn.

The baron appeared surprised that she would even ask. "But of course." He shrugged. "A man situated as I am is not in need of any other kind! Alas, my uncle—"

"Enjoys remarkable health," Frederica supplied.

The baron nodded. "He refuses to die. And my creditors—"

"Refuse, I imagine, to die also."

The baron smiled. "Refuse to die and demand to be paid. They've become as convinced as I am that the old lord is immortal, and are no longer willing to wait for me to come into his fortune."

"So." It was the dry tone again. "You have decided to seek a fortune of your own. Or . . ." The lady thought. "Of *my* own."

The baron nodded. "You understand me very well, Lady Frederica. I have always liked that about you. The other heiresses in London this season—none of them understands me as you do. And not even for money did I think I could bear marrying one or two of them. Take Miss Fulton, for instance . . . " He seemed lost in the discussion, and Frederica decided it was best to let him talk, reasoning that while he was talking he was doing nothing else. "I am sure that at this very moment Miss Fulton would be treating me to a case of hysterics never before witnessed in the history of man, but there you sit, calm and collected, as if you've just come for tea." The word rang a mental bell and he gazed inquiringly at her. "By the way, my dear, may I offer you a cup of tea?"

"Do not," Frederica said, each word final, "call me that."

For a moment the baron's forehead wrinkled, then he smiled. "I will not," he promised. "Now. About that tea . . ."

Frederica made it clear that she did not intend to sip a sip or eat a bite in his company; the baron, shrugging, said that she must do what she thought best, but . . . it was a long way to Scotland.

There was a scratching at the door, and Frederica, whose heart had plunged when he confirmed their Gretna Green destination, looked hopefully toward the sound. Her hopes were blighted seconds later as the baron, understanding the look, said, "I am sorry to disappoint you, my dear, but you will only waste your energy should you try to escape or seek help from the landlord here. He is in my employ and can be quite deaf when necessary."

Frederica raised an eyebrow. "Come here often, do you, Baron Barnsley?" she asked.

He laughed.

The landlord had brought food, a mug of ale for the baron and a pitcher of milk—milk!—for the lady. Frederica's companion sat at the small table lit by the tallow candles, enjoying his meal. She had declined his invitation to join him, remaining by the fire, her face turned stonily away. Watching her, Barnsley sighed and said, "I don't know if it will make any difference to you, Lady Frederica, but I fancied myself much in love with Eliza Marchand."

Frederica sniffed. "And a fine way you had of showing it too!"

The baron's tone was almost penitent as he agreed. "She was so lovely," he said. "I wanted to show her Paris and Rome. How was I to know all she wanted was an estate in Yorkshire with a passel of brats giggling at her feet?"

"You might have asked her."

The baron shrugged. "Yes," he agreed, "I might have. It never occurred to me."

"I'm sure!"

The baron smiled. "So," he said, "let me rectify that mistake on this elopement. Tell me, Lady Frederica—what do you want?"

"We," the lady said, her chin high, "are not eloping. And what I want is to go home."

The baron shook his head. "It grieves me to disappoint you, my lady. But we *are* eloping. And you will not be going home again until your name is Barnsley." He watched her for several moments, then said, the question abrupt, "After all, this is what you wanted, isn't it? To be married?"

"I—" She was surprised. He watched her school her features with effort. "I don't know what you mean!"

"No," the baron agreed, the words slow, "I'm not sure, either. But anyone who believes you became engaged to Viscount Chilesworth out of love must have pudding for brains! So you must wish to be married—perhaps because of our earlier encounter in Hyde Park? Perhaps your father thought marriage would offer you stability and a protective name?" He gave his most engaging grin at her gasp, realizing he had guessed aright. "Come now, Lady Frederica! We can both give each other what we wish! I will give you my name, and my promise not to be too careful a husband. You can go your own way and I—"

"Will go straight through my money," Frederica finished for him. Not for the world did she intend to tell him she did not want someone who would not be a careful husband.

The baron nodded. "Would it be such a bad bargain?"

Frederica's head moved up and down. It would, she told him; it would indeed. She, herself, could not like any agreement that started with kidnapping.

"Elopement," the baron protested. "It has a better ring. And speaking of rings . . . I have something here I thought you might like . . ." He walked to the chair on which he had thrown his greatcoat and rummaged in the pockets there. For a moment his back was to her, and Frederica took full advantage of that. Snatching up the pottery pitcher of milk brought for her, she crept up behind him and was raising the pitcher as the baron started to turn toward her. She brought the pitcher down with haste, and the baron crumpled forward.

"No one," she informed his unconscious body as she dusted her hands with satisfaction and moved back so the rivulets of milk would not soil her gown further, "kidnaps Frederica Farthingham."

She sped to the door and was out it in a second, closing it softly behind her just as a voice said, *"Frederica!"*

The lady thought she would jump out of her skin as she whirled at this new sound, only to find her betrothed and her brother standing several feet from her. Both had serviceable swords hanging at their sides.

"Anthony," she cried, throwing herself forward before she even thought of what she did. "Oh, Anthony!" Her arms went around his neck, and one of Chilesworth's arms curled protectively about her body. His other hand fingered his sword with menace.

"And George!" Frederica removed herself from her betrothed's chest and cast herself upon her brother's. "Good old George!" She was surprised to find she was crying, and stepped back from her brother's quick embrace to wipe her eyes.

"I am so g-g-*glad* to see you both!" she cried. "And I've gone and g-g-gotten *milk* all over you!"

Both men looked down to where the milk that had splashed on Frederica when she bashed the baron had been transferred by her embraces to their coats.

"Milk?" Chilesworth said, touching one of the spots and holding his wet finger to his lips to taste.

George ignored the milk and took Frederica's upper arms in a painful grip as he asked, his voice hard and his eyes anxious, "Are you all right, Freddie? Has he hurt you in any way?"

"No, George!" she said. "I am fine. Really."

Her brother gave her a slight shake. "Then why are you crying?"

"Because, George"—she fell forward onto his chest again—"I am just so h-h-*happy* to see you!" Her words made her think, and she pulled back to look up at one and then the other.

"What *are* you doing here, George?" she demanded.

"What—" her brother replied, exchanging glances with Anthony. They both looked at her in surprise. "Why, we've come to rescue you, of course."

"Oh!" Frederica favored each with a wide smile. "That is very good of you, I'm sure. But I have already rescued myself!" She put a hand on each man's arm. "So let us go home. At once!" Frederica started forward, but the figures beside her refused to move.

"No, Frederica," Chilesworth said, and his voice sounded so like his father's that Frederica shivered. "This time I do not mean to leave until my business with Baron Barnsley is finished."

"But Anthony . . ." She shuddered at the way he said

finished and put both her hands around his arm as he started forward. "You cannot!"

"What?" Chilesworth frowned down at her. "What do you mean, I cannot? You don't have some tender feeling for this fellow, do you, because—"

Frederica made it clear that any feelings she had for the baron were *far* from tender, but above her indignation floated a threat from her conversation with Anthony's father. The baron, the earl had said, was an excellent swordsman. "He might kill you!" she cried.

The viscount's face grew darker. "I thank you for that vote of confidence."

Frederica looked for help from George, but he seemed just as determined as Anthony to be ridiculous. "Well, it makes no difference if you kill him or he kills you," she said, hurrying along between them as the two approached the door behind which she'd left the baron. "Either way you'll be gone."

"What?" Both her brother and Chilesworth looked surprised.

"You know dueling is illegal, Anthony!" she cried. "If you kill Barnsley, you will have to flee."

"She's right, you know." George was growing thoughtful.

Frederica rushed on. "Besides," she said, "you can't fight a man who is already wounded."

"What?" Chilesworth shook off her hand and thrust open the door. He and George stopped at sight of the baron, lying where Frederica had left him on the floor, puddles of milk and shards of pottery surrounding his wet form. Fearing for a moment that she had done more damage than she thought, Frederica watched her brother approach Barnsley, and whispered, "He—he isn't dead, is he, George?"

George shook his head. "No," he said, "and more's the pity!"

"George!"

Both men looked at her, questions in their eyes, and Frederica flushed. "I would not like to be a murderess," she said. George was frowning down at the broken pieces of pitcher surrounding the baron.

"What happened here, Freddie?" he asked.

"Frederica," she corrected. "And I hit him with a pitcher." They were looking stunned, and, trying to explain, she continued, "A pitcher of milk."

"Hit him . . ." George looked up and seemed to struggle with himself as a reluctant gleam appeared in his eye. "She hit him with a pitcher of milk," he informed the viscount. Glancing at the wet floor, the gleam grew. "A full pitcher, I'd say." Frederica nodded, but Chilesworth frowned. It was apparent Anthony saw nothing funny in the statement.

"Don't you understand, Anthony?" George asked, rising from his place by the baron's inert body and coming forward to put a hand on his friend's shoulder. "She hit him with a pitcher of milk!"

"She should not have had to hit him with anything!"

"Last time . . ." George chortled. "Last time he got hit with a door. . . ."

"I fail to see—" Chilesworth began, then did see. In spite of himself, he smiled.

"The baron," George said, "has a habit of kidnapping the wrong women."

Yes, the viscount agreed, his hand bidding a reluctant farewell to his sword handle. Yes, the baron certainly did.

Frederica, glaring at them, said it was wrong to kidnap anyone, and if they were done being ridiculous, she would like to go home.

Chapter
Twenty-Four

"*DRAT!*"

It was the third time the earring had slipped through Frederica's fingers, and she gazed at it in consternation as it rolled across the floor and came to rest at the foot of a delicate Queen Anne chair that stood three feet away from the small dressing table at which she sat. A grinning Jane chased after the errant earring, pausing to flash a knowing smile at her mistress as she stopped to pick it up.

"Now, Lady Frederica," the maid soothed, walking the few steps back to the dressing table to drop the earring into Frederica's hand, "there's no reason to be nervous, I'm sure—"

Frederica dropped the earring again. "N-n-nervous?" she echoed. The good-natured Jane picked up the small sapphire and diamond concoction, and carefully fitted it into her mistress's ear. "I-I don't know what you mean!"

Jane gave a skillful tug at the small curl she wanted to fall forward over Frederica's shoulder, and rearranged the diamond and sapphire hairclip in Frederica's hair more to her liking. Picking up the elegant nosegay of violets edged in silver paper and tied up with long blue ribbons that matched the color of Frederica's gown to perfection, the maid handed the flowers to the lady and beamed.

"Oh, Lady Frederica!" she breathed. "It's beautiful you are, to be sure!"

Frederica, turning to the full-length mirror that stood across the room, stared uncomprehendingly at the young woman gazing solemnly back at her. Madame Chautinand had outdone herself, and the gown Frederica wore set off her small figure in a way guaranteed to dazzle a great many of those attending the ball that evening. The tiny silvery flowers of the blue gauze overskirt caught the light of several candles that lit her room and gave her a shimmering appearance that, Jane said, fair took her breath away. The paper and ribbons of Anthony's nosegay, which had arrived that afternoon with a prettily worded note saying he hoped she would carry these as she carried his heart, so exactly matched the silver and blue of the gown that Frederica, fingering the flowers with tenderness, felt her eyes mist.

That was not unusual; ever since the flowers arrived, Frederica had felt an almost overwhelming urge to burst into tears each time she looked at them. Glancing away from her reflection, she was surprised to see Jane, her face wreathed in smiles, coming toward her with a box she held with great care.

"From your mama and your papa," Jane said, delivering the message just as it had been given to her. "With love."

"Wha—" Frederica began, taking the box and walking with it to the bed. Putting it down she looked at the maid in surprise, then opened the lid to find a silver gauze scarf of such exquisite workmanship that she was almost afraid to lift it, for fear the fine material would drift apart.

"Jane!" Frederica said, eyes wide. "It's—it's—"

"It's to carry crooked through your elbows, my lady," the maid supplied, hurrying forward. "Your mama said that French woman recommended it when you were in her shop. See how the silver matches that of the flowers in your gown? And"—her smile grew—"that pretty paper that wraps up his lordship's violets."

"It's beautiful," Frederica said, standing still as the busy maid draped it over her arms.

"Yes, my lady," the maid said, gently leading her mistress back to the long mirror.

"Just beautiful," Frederica said.

Jane was considerably startled when tears suddenly poured down her lady's cheeks. "Now, Lady Frederica," Jane began, making an ineffectual daub at the tears. "It will be all right."

"It won't," Frederica cried. "Oh, Jane, how can it? When everyone has been so good, and Anthony sent violets—violets are my favorite, Jane, you know that!" The maid gave a sympathetic nod as Frederica's words tumbled on. "And he is . . . *resigned*!"

The thought of his lordship's resignation—to what, Jane did not know—seemed to set her mistress's tears flowing faster, and the maid was much relieved when a soft knock on the door was followed a moment later by the appearance of Frederica's mother, who had come to see if her daughter was ready to go down to greet the guests who would be joining them for dinner before the ball. The countess, making a quick assessment of the situation, sent the confused maid out of the room and set herself to soothing her daughter with a "Come now, Frederica! This will not do!"

"Mama!" Frederica raised a tearstained but resolute face to her mother. "I cannot marry Anthony!"

The countess, who had a much better idea than Frederica why that statement seemed to make her daughter cry harder, patted Frederica's shoulder and said, "Oh, can't you now?"

Frederica's head moved from side to side. "No."

"Well," the countess said with a sigh, "I suppose if you can't, you can't."

"*What?*" The word came out on an arrested sob, and Frederica gazed at Lady Forkham in surprise. "*What*, Mama?"

Lucinda appeared inordinately interested in the contents of Frederica's dressing table. "I suppose if you can't marry him, you can't marry him," the countess repeated.

"But . . ." Frederica did not waste time trying to understand why her mother had made this drastic about-face, or why the countess's words distressed her even further. "But . . . you and Papa said—"

Lady Forkham turned an inquiring gaze upon her daughter and Frederica gulped. "Aren't you going to . . . command me to marry Anthony, Mama?" she asked.

The countess smiled. "My dear," she said, "I do not believe commanding is very much in my line."

"But Papa—" Frederica began.

Lady Forkham's smile disappeared. "Ah, yes," she said. She appeared to be deep in thought. "Your father. Your father is another matter."

Frederica felt something like hope building, only to have the countess dash it down again. "Well," Lady Forkham said, checking her own gown in the long mirror and avoiding looking at her daughter, "I suppose you will have to tell him."

"What?"

Lucinda looked at her in surprise. "But, Frederica," she said, "it seems only fair!"

"I—I—I *cannot!*" Frederica wailed.

"I think you should tell Manningham, too, of course," Lady Forkham said, giving the question due consideration. "And Anthony. Although"—she slanted a speculative glance at her daughter—"perhaps Anthony will not be as disappointed."

That thought did not seem to give Frederica joy. If anything, her face fell further, and she said, turning away, "I cannot, Mama! I cannot go downstairs."

The countess's eyebrows rose. "Whyever not?" she asked.

"I cannot face them—" Frederica stopped, surprised at her mother's trill of laughter.

"My love," Lady Forkham said, her smile fond, "a woman who can floor a kidnapper with a pitcher of milk can face your father and Manningham and Chilesworth, I'm sure!"

"But—"

"You owe it to them, Frederica." Her mother's voice was gentle but firm. "You really do."

Frederica, about to protest, met her mother's eyes and gave a slow nod. Yes, she supposed she did. Standing with the tragic pose of one about to go to the guillotine, she allowed the countess to rearrange the curls that had fallen forward in her distraction, to twitch the lovely silver gauze shawl into place, to hand her the delicate violet nosegay, and to take one of Frederica's unresisting hands and lead her to her fate.

"There," the countess whispered, for all the world like a conspirator as she gazed about the room and pointed Frederica's attention toward the four men gathered in a corner. Only Frederica's Great-aunt Honoria, Anthony, and his mother and father had arrived yet. Aunt Honoria and the Countess of Manningham sat near the fire, exchanging pleasantries, and Anthony and his father, along with Frederica's father and her brother, George, stood talking and laughing together. Just as her eyes found him Frederica saw Anthony throw his head back and laugh, and her throat tightened. How happy he seemed! If only . . .

A look of such wistfulness crossed Frederica's face that her mother almost pulled her from the room and tried to tell her the home truths that the countess had decided Frederica would understand only if she discovered them for herself. Before she could weaken further, Lucinda gave Frederica a shove forward and a bright, encouraging smile.

Frederica cast one last pleading glance over her shoulder,

then, straightening her backbone, she walked forward. "Papa . . ." she began just as her father saw her and came forward to take her hand.

"Ah, Frederica," Forkham cried, "there you are! And looking quite beautiful, if a proud father is allowed to say such things!"

The other men turned, and Frederica saw the warm light rush into Anthony's eyes. "Beautiful," he seconded as George and Manningham added their confirmation. She flushed and looked away, and instantly the viscount's eyes narrowed.

"Frederica," Chilesworth said, taking a step toward her, "what is it?"

She put out a hand as if to ward him off, and he stopped, the light in his eyes disappearing. "Anthony . . ." she said. Her voice sounded desperate, even to her own ears. "Papa, my lord . . ." She raised her eyes to Manningham's and lowered them, for he stood as still as his son, their expressions almost identical. "I must speak to you!"

"But of course," her father said. "Say whatever you like."

Behind her, Frederica heard Higgins announce the arrival of the Butteringtons, and she said, her voice almost a squeak, "Alone!"

"What—" Her father frowned, aware that something was amiss but not sure what. George, touching the earl's shoulder, suggested that he, Manningham, Chilesworth, and Frederica repair to the library while George and his mother greeted their new guests.

"But—" Forkham began; he was overrode by Manningham, who said in a colorless voice that only increased Frederica's misery, that he thought that a very good idea. With a small bow Manningham indicated that Frederica should lead the way and that the three of them would follow.

They walked in silence to the library, Manningham

opening the door for Frederica when it seemed his son, who stood at her shoulder, could do no more than stare down at her with those hard eyes that tried their best to will her to look up at him. The lady kept her gaze fixed on the floor until they were inside the room; then she raised an agitated face to her father's and said, her voice shaking, "Papa, I cannot marry Anthony!"

Manningham watched as his son's hands knotted and unknotted at his side, his face growing still.

"*What?*" Forkham roared more than said the word, and Frederica flinched.

"Do not, my lord," said a quiet voice from Forkham's left, and Frederica's father swung his gaze toward Chilesworth.

"*What?*"

"Do not shout at her, I beg."

"*Shout?*" It was apparent that Forkham intended to do so; in fact, the purpling of his face suggested he intended to do a great *deal* of shouting. "*Shout,* sir? When my house is to be filled this evening with over four hundred people, all come to hear of the engagement of my daughter to yourself, and now my daughter says—says—and you ask me not to *shout*?" Forkham glared from the viscount to Frederica, then back again. "Well, I *will* shout, sir! I will shout all I like!"

"Papa!" Frederica was very white, but she stood her ground as her father's glare returned to her. "You must not take this out on Anthony. It is not his fault—"

"Not—" Forkham's mouth opened and shut several times. "Not—" He was having trouble getting his words out. "Then whose fault is it, I'd like to know? And why did you wait until now to tell me, when the two of you have been getting on thick as thieves all the time these past weeks, and we thought—we thought—"

"Papa, don't!" Frederica said, turning her head away. Chilesworth took a step toward her, then stopped.

Once again Manningham saw his son's fists ball at his side and said, his voice a complaining drawl, "I take it, Anthony, that you did not take my advice."

"What?" The word, rapped out, was automatic as Chilesworth's gaze, along with those of Frederica and her father, transferred to Manningham.

"Really, dear boy." Manningham removed a nonexistent piece of fluff from his sleeve before raising his bored glance to his son's. "I *told* you it is considered polite form to tell your betrothed that you love her. I thought you would have had the wisdom to do so. It is quite tiresome of you not to have done so."

A dull red flush crept up Chilesworth's neck, but it was Frederica who replied with an impassioned "But he does *not* love me!"

"*What?*" The word, incredulous, came from the viscount, and Frederica, surprised, could only stare at him for a moment before turning away.

"You don't," she mourned, the words tragic as she shrugged off the hand he moved to place on her shoulder. "You said you are—are—"

"*Resigned*, I believe was the word," Manningham supplied, removing yet another piece of nonexistent lint. Two pairs of young eyes, one hurt and one impatient, were directed toward Anthony's parent before Chilesworth again placed his hand on Frederica's shoulder and turned her around to face him.

"Freddie," he began, the word so tender that at the sound of it tears started to flow down her cheeks.

"F-F-Frederica," she cried. "And I—I—"

Manningham sighed. "You love him too much to marry him if he is only 'resigned'?" he supplied. Frederica, dismayed, tried to deny it, could not, and nodded, turning her head away.

"Really, Father!" Chilesworth was exasperated. "I believe I asked you before to allow me to conduct my own courtship—"

"And such a good job you've done of it too," Manningham said.

Chilesworth's brows snapped together, and he ignored his father as he turned his full attention to the small figure before him. "Frederica," he began, taking her in his arms, "do you?"

She gave a watery sniff, refusing to look up at him. "Do I what?"

"What my father said—" he began.

"Love him," Manningham interjected, rolling his eyes. The viscount frowned at him.

"Well . . ." She chanced a quick glance up, noting as she did so that her father was standing off to the side, looking for all the world like someone who had wandered unexpectedly into Bedlam and was seeking desperately for the way out. She almost chuckled, even as she said, "I—that is—" She looked up again.

"Do *you*?" she demanded.

"Do I what?" Now it was the viscount's turn to ask.

"What your father said—"

"*Love* her, Anthony." Manningham was growing impatient and thanking his lucky stars he never had to be as young as these children again. "For goodness sake, do you *love* her?"

"I believe, sir," the earl's son snapped, not at all pleased with his father's help, "that we could dispense with your presence. And that of Forkham, too!"

"Now see here—" Frederica's father began; he did not like being dismissed in his own home. He stopped, however, when Manningham touched his arm and inclined his head toward the door, indicating they should go.

"Very well," Forkham grumbled, "but what this is all about—"

"I'll explain it to you," Frederica and Anthony heard

Manningham say as he walked toward the door. He paused a moment on the threshold to add, his eyes upon them, "It is a rather funny story, really, and one that I believe"—he quirked an eyebrow in inquiry—"has a happy ending?"

The viscount nodded at his sire and the earl smiled.

"You must forgive him, my dear," Manningham said, addressing Frederica, who did not look up. "He cannot help being an idiot."

"Father!" Chilesworth said in protest as the door closed behind the earl. Balked of that target, he turned his attention to the lady, who stood unmoving beside him. It seemed only natural to take her into his arms, and he did, one hand moving up to cradle her neck as with the other he raised her chin and said, "Frederica, please . . ."

Her lips parted slightly, and she gave a small gasp of surprise at the tenderness in his face. "Please?" she repeated.

"You mustn't desert me now, my darling. Not after all we've been through!"

"But . . ." Her eyes widened. "Then what your father said . . . is true?"

The viscount's head moved up and down, coming closer and closer to her own. For a moment Chilesworth's lips grazed hers. "When I realized you were gone," he said, "at the masquerade, it was as if my world had disappeared, as if there were a large piece of ice inside me, growing and growing, and I was afraid that we would not rescue you in time—"

"But, Anthony," she protested, "you did not have to rescue me."

He grinned. "Yes, my heart's delight," he said. His thumb was having a mesmerizing effect on her neck, Frederica decided; something about the rubbing action there was turning her knees weak. "But I did not know you were so deadly with a pitcher of milk!"

"Then you *do* wish to marry me?" It was said with such

incredulity that the viscount could not credit it; he drew back in amazement and, the words heartfelt, said that he wished it above all else.

"And you?" His thumb was making those dangerous circles again. "Why did you try to cry off, Frederica? I thought . . . I hoped—"

"You said you were *resigned*!" she told him, striking his chest with one small hand as she suddenly glared up at him. "*Resigned* to marry me! Well, I did not wish to wed a man *resigned* to being my husband! *Resigned*! Indeed!" She gave one of the small sniffs that were such a part of her, and Chilesworth, relieved, threw back his head and laughed.

"Ah, Freddie!" he said. His lips traced the place along her neck where his thumb had so recently been, then moved up her cheek to her mouth, where they rested several long moments before he pulled back to smile down at her.

"You love me!" she said, for once forgetting to correct his use of her childhood name.

The viscount smiled. "I do." He lifted her hand to his lips and the color of his eyes deepened. "And you?"

Frederica gulped. "Why—" she began, then stopped. "Why, I suppose I love you too!"

The engagement ball for the Lady Frederica Farthingham and Viscount Chilesworth was, everyone said, a sad crush—the saddest of the season, which made it London's largest success. The lady seemed to float on her betrothed's arm, and more than one member of the opposite sex ground his or her teeth to see how the two smiled at each other, as if they'd just discovered something no one else knew.

Which, the Earl and Countess of Forkham and the Earl and Countess of Manningham thought, watching them with a great deal of satisfaction, it was just possible they had.